The Rose Rabbi

The

Rose Rabbi

by

Daniel Stern

McGRAW-HILL BOOK COMPANY
New York   St. Louis   San Francisco   Dusseldorf
Mexico   Toronto

THE ROSE RABBI

Library of Congress Catalog Card Number: 75-161847

First Edition

07-061203-x

Gloria

The Rose Rabbi

Chapter 1. ALL men are artists. After all, they have their lives.

Perhaps that is why on the morning of my fortieth birthday I decided to forcibly and actually recapture my earlier life. Even before I was completely awake I was in the past rehearsing old defeats. It started with the sleepy remembered sound of a piece for string orchestra I'd once written. Yes, I was a musician before I became a kind of businessman. But although it was a gentle, proud piece for strings, it was connected with a remembered humiliation.

I'd taken a piece, a Pastorale for String Orchestra, to Henry Crown for criticism. No! What lunatic would ask for criticism? Rather, I asked for approval, for celebration. Crown and I walked in Central Park—the Central Park of years ago, which was itself a kind of Pastorale for Strings, particularly at my age which was twenty-two. And also, bear in mind that this was Henry Crown, a composer, heroically self-proclaimed; winner of our high school's Music Award for his Dirge for Kafka. A man whose life, at twenty-three, was already encased in capital letters. I was strictly lower-case.

Through the park we stumbled—he fat, myself thin—chasing our future reputations. Finally, after glancing over my score, Crown took the paper and rubbed it on the grass until green smears interspersed the notes.

"Wolf," he said, "there's your Pastorale." And we said no more about it, going on to years of friendship, anger and separation; to my attempts at writing, which failed so unhappily, and my attempts at business, which succeeded so well, ending up in my extraordinary position, through which you may have heard of me: Wolf Walker, Ethical Advisor to the Lester & French Advertising Agency.

I lay long listening to the pulse of those strings, broken years ago, until the alarm clock reminded me what year it was. Then I rose to explore the day of my birth, the apartment of my year-old marriage, the city of my youth and maturity. And what a city! Two abandoned universities in my own neighborhood, one to the north and one only a few blocks away, all study left to cobwebs and small, scurrying beings. Hunger strikers had infiltrated every corner of the city. One came across their empty gaze at unexpected turns: a daily reproach. The suburbs were sprinkled with semilegal academies in which the philosophical and practical aspects of self-destruction were explored in seclusion (though the recent rash of child-suicides had brought a crackdown from the authorities and there were rumors that the academies were being quietly discontinued). And, while the city flourished in its ripening parks and decaying concrete webs, automobile graveyards appeared, at least one in every section, where people brought their hopeless car wrecks and left them to rust and crumble through the seasons.

Still, the distant wars thrived and business went on as usual. Along with the secret hope of improvement: of one's living conditions, of one's own spirit, of one's job. Marriages still worked or split, as always. And the spring sunshine was cool and clear this year; the freeze of the winter was over, the blasting heat of the summer was still to come. The chilly floor mottled with sun and shadow led me through the bedroom toward a deserted apartment. My wife's bedroom slippers were two tufted guardians at her side of the bed. She had left me alone on this pivotal day to travel three thousand miles on a mercy mission on behalf of her father's genitalia. Age. Prostates. Painful urination. In spite of his amateur anti-Semitism, my father-in-law deserved better.

Did I tell you my wife was not Jewish? Blonde but intense. The absence she left in the apartment this morning was like a presence. I pushed it ahead of me into the bathroom where it was further enriched by the unfilled half of a lipstick, a reddened Kleenex and an eyebrow pencil. I registered these lightly as temporary emblems of departure (and implied return). But only lightly. My mind was embedded, still, in that half-light, that blur of remembered images that belong neither to sleep nor to the waking day. It concealed a peculiar crew—dominated by the round but far from benign figure of Henry Crown and accompanied by the pulverized Pastorale for Strings. These fugitive images included Stacey, a red-haired modern dancer with whom I'd lived in the Village before it split into East and West like Germany (and like Stacey and myself), a red souvenir of my radical days. And Barton Bester was there, somewhere, the other dominant force of my early days: Communist, cocksman, and now owner of a chain of restaurants thought to be backed by the Mafia. Thus, the crowded romance of my early-morning preconscious. I played with it, refused to give it up, glazing my eyes with half-distorted memories. Still, they were alert enough to notice a neat little red notebook with a blue fleur-de-lis on the cover next to my wife's forgotten eyebrow pencil. I flipped it open and saw the words, . . . *"late . . . if it's true I must do something about it right away . . ."*

• • •

Chapter 2. I WAS wide awake at once. A painful birthday, humiliated Pastorale memories, and now the realization that my wife kept some kind of a diary of which I knew nothing. And in that diary was a notation that seemed to indicate she was pregnant and was to have an abortion. Or did it? Words before and after the shocking statement were scratched out with heavy strokes of a felt pen. *Late*— that could only mean one thing. The red tides of the moon, as Barton Bester used to call menstruation. And if that *was* the sense of the word "late," then the other sentence could only mean that my wife was off in California—under cover of the false mission of her father's prostate crisis—to have my child carved from her womb and discarded like a piece of failed sculpture. A genital journey, but female masquerading as male.

It was the only notation on the page. I closed the little book and stared at the pale blue fleur-de-lis. I knew I was not going to turn any other pages. Tag-ends of rabbinical tales and talmudic references to prying, peeking, and the right of privacy trickled through my brain. They nibbled at me, but I could not split so far away from what I'd become. I wanted to look and learn precisely what Carla had meant by the one cryptic phrase I'd read. But I'd gone through so many rhapsodic justifications of the rabbinic function— more, of the entire ethical mode of perceiving and dealing with reality—that I was under extraordinary constraints.

Carla on the other hand, leaned toward the unstructured —loose and lovely she would lie under my mouth and dare me to flower into something beyond the ethical.

· 4 ·

"Take a chance, Wolf," she'd say. "Play a hunch; obey a whim. Something unexpectedly pleasant."

"I do." I murmured, "all the time. But not where serious things are concerned."

I hated the stuffy centuries that echoed behind my words. Imaginary earlocks tickled my cheeks.

"Jews are so—so stiff-necked."

"Gentiles are so—so blond," I said into the yellow disorder of her hair.

"No, don't laugh out of it!" she cried.

And I would be off again, explaining the value of applying systems to moral problems.

"You're just defending your job."

"I got the job because I think this way—not vice versa."

"You're just defending the Jews."

"Listen, have you told your old man I'm Jewish, yet?"

"Jews are so damned good!"

I rolled off the bed, pushed by the force of the word.

"Ridiculous! I never said that!"

But of course by everything I did I affirmed the truth of it, or the belief in it, stated or unstated. (There was the famous incident of Crown, Bester, and the girl I'd refused to share. Carla often teased me with it.) And it *was* a foolish position to be in, placing me, as well, in the further foolishness of not being able to exercise small, sweet sins such as reading Carla's private diary. *Late . . . must do something . . .*

The talks became arguments, the arguments fights, and the fights a kind of summing up of Carla's critical sense of who I was and how I lived—all of it, apparently, an attack on her.

"What do you think would be so different if we lived out there in the sun?" I asked.

"Your eyes might open."

"They are open! I can see you."

She followed me to the floor and traced imaginary stripes down my stomach.

"No, baby, Jews look inside—insight, I think you call it. Comes from living in cities."

The few totally verifiable facts I knew about Carla all added up to a single image: one big eye, that was how she was represented to me whenever I closed my eyes to imagine her. (She was right about the insight versus outsight.) She had been a photographer of animals, photographing tigers for natural history museums, as well as for gasoline ads representing power, or flights of snowy egrets representing peace. California, apparently, was blessed with both power and peace and Carla had been an observing eye on the natural world before coming to New York and closer horizons. Her eye extended backward in time, as well. A great-grandfather had made optical instruments for her grand-uncle who had been optician to the King of Denmark. Her older brother was a retoucher who wielded an air-brush as if it were an exquisite paint brush on canvas. Two of her uncles were painters. She came from a long line of eyes; whereas I apprehended the world through sound, to her it poured into retina and cornea to be, not translated, but directly perceived.

"You listen," she complained, "all the time."

"Why, do you think?"

"Because fine distinctions—and you are in the fine-distinctions business—are heard, not seen."

"One *draws* distinctions," I said.

She ignored that and said, "Close your eyes and imagine a Rabbi receiving the problems of a believer—or nonbeliever for that matter."

"Okay . . ."

"The Rabbi's eyes could just as well be closed as open.

· 6 ·

Perhaps even better closed. The moral sense is un-visual. The eye cures, cleans, and speaks directly. The ear opens up all kinds of ambiguities. It's why hypnosis is performed with the subject's eyes shut. Hypnosis is amoral."

"Is that why you haven't let me hypnotize you for so long?"

"You may not have the knack any more," she laughed. And I let the issue pass for the moment, for I had once taken great pleasure in hypnotizing women. Women in general, before I was married, and Carla in particular, afterward.

But she would not be put off. "We're opposites," she said. "Morality is vision without eyes—a paradox. Seeing is, after all, only literal. You can only see what's there. The moral tone can catch all kinds of things from the invisible world." This was a voice of hers I'd never heard before. Scholarly and a touch poetic. In the year we'd been married, I'd caught no single, genuine voice of her own.

The arguments continued in varying forms and different intensities; all of them had much the same content: Carla was pulling me away from my dead, New York Jewish work to some mythical California of the spirit where everyone experienced life directly, without intermediaries (no ethical advisors), under the sun and away from the cities of darkness.

Chapter 3. ALL marriages have something of the sort running through them. Every woman thinks her man is either too spiritual or too physical, too abstract or too realistic. But for the most part we lived like an average married couple; each of us quite mysterious to the other underneath the realism of daily life. My background at the seminary, and the wandering, broke days afterward were opaque to her. Her days tracking down lions and leopards in a station wagon, a camera in her hand, her nights filled with similarly savage affairs, brief and entirely physical (or so I chose to imagine), were, in a deep sense, unimaginable. We met on the neutral ground of the present and the future. Which may be one reason why the past grew to be more and more of an obsession to me.

And so, to try and tell the untellable, the texture of our days: we lived together, that year of the shared city, in the up-and-down mystery of the day-to-day. Partly living in the present, artist friends who frequented a painters' bar downtown and had a special feeling for the drugs of the day; getting to know Burns, the account executive I worked with, at long, drunken dinners during which he revealed to us the latest chapter in his religious crisis: The Pope was fallible, the Pope was infallible—and, finally, when the Pope resigned, what a dinner that was! He didn't show up at work for a week afterward, and when he did, refused to discuss religion or related topics again.

Weaving in and out of those days was the pendulum of recollection; the kind of exploration people do during courtship, but with Carla and myself it seemed to thread itself out permanently. There was always a new recollection, or a gloss, a commentary on an old one. Her father, the only relative she saw or cared for, took shape gradually in my mind: American as rock, ballsy as ever as he entered his seventh decade, and convinced as ever that the cause of most of the world's troubles could be traced to the Jews. I never got it straight from Carla if he knew I was Jewish or not. But he kept his three-thousand-mile distance, leaving us to discover ourselves; Carla drifting from marginal job to marginal job, neither of us quite coming to grips with the question of children.

Did I tell you that she was much younger than I? Precisely: twenty-five years old. Perhaps that was what made that first year so complex, ending in my chase down the years. We had been to almost every city in Europe on our honeymoon. Then, all during the next twelve months strange letters kept arriving: a check for a thousand dollars from Holland, a pamphlet that promised to prove how the Jews had been responsible for World War II, the planning of World War III, The War of the Roses, and many other calamities. Then recordings of pieces by Mahler, Sibelius, Delius, Elgar, Grieg—the names seemed tied together by some sinister, unrecognizable pattern. Until I realized, from a casual remark dropped by Carla, that they were simply all second-rate. Not one piece by Beethoven or Schubert or Bach among them. (I tried, desperately, to remember if I had told her of my conversation with Crown about my Pastorale and his subsequent warnings of the dangers of a second-rate life in art. But I couldn't be sure.) Then, a folder containing the first six lessons of a course in Portuguese. Did Carla have escape plans to Brazil in the first months after our marriage?

She denied everything by laughing or looking at me steadily. Then she would return to the Malayan Breathing System which absorbed her for a time. All I really knew about her was the present. What she said to me while making love, how she looked curled up like a lovely, long-haired, blonde serpent doing her breathing exercises; and all her skin creams and perfumes, most of them with Asian names: Breath of the East, Kashmir Scent. Yet, Carla herself had a rather neutral smell, fresh and young—unused.

Two nights before my birthday she had given me my present, a new expensive edition of the Babylonian Talmud.

Later, we'd made love on the living room couch. Before each of us goes off on one of our infrequent solo trips, myself on business, Carla to visit her family in Los Angeles, we make love. The idea, though never verbalized, is clearly to take the sexual edge off the traveling partner.

Lying in my arms, she was a tangle of long blonde hair. Winking under my right eye was a very pink nipple. She sighed, a sound I interpreted as satisfaction. But it turned out otherwise.

"I wish I wasn't going to be away on your birthday."

"Don't go."

"Cruel. My father's an old man. Alone and sick."

"It's not so great being a young man alone and well."

"You did it for a long time."

"That's why I have no taste for loneliness now."

"Come with me."

"Can't. The Bester restaurant account is still hanging in the air."

"I meant—come for good."

She stirred against me.

"I read that Bester is opening a chain of restaurants in L.A.," she said. A tricky shift.

I squinted down at her blond crown. "He's expanding too fast—the money *has* to be coming from somewhere."

"Banks?"

"Or Mafia."

"Not Barton Bester. A nice Jewish boy like that."

"Don't make the gentile mistake of thinking all Jews are alike."

"California's a great place for bringing up children." Double tricky shift. Silence filled the room along with the regular hiss of our respiration. It was a moment of mystery: the question of children, of having them or not, of Carla's past history of pregnancy or abortions or narrow escapes. All the procreative details remained a mystery. Every time the notion arrived that we ought to think about having a child, it somehow receded into ambiguity often after a period of trying; or was it merely a period of taking chances, of carelessness? It could never be pinned down.

And in her loose-limbed, limp-styled way she was still a child herself. The day I'd met her was also the last time I'd seen Henry Crown. She was his date—at a Composers' Society concert. Their manner toward each other seemed both cool and intense. I found out her number and called her the next day and we were married four months later. As to how long they'd been going out together, the nature of their relationship: mystery. I respected her reticence. I had my own, holding back some of the deep sources of my discontent: music, writing, my daily struggle with the Ethical Factory. Her reticence was of the West Coast variety, all cool, vague, and unfocused. Mine was Eastern: intense, secretive, potentially explosive. Some day perhaps we would have a child and the mystery would be solved. (Perhaps she knew she couldn't have a child and wanted to spare me the news.) My mind invented story after story. Crown had knocked her up and the inevitable abortion had been bungled in old-movie style leaving her damaged internally. Or, she couldn't bear the idea of a Jewish child either for good or bad reasons. Good reason: Jews suffer. Bad reason: her father didn't want Jewish grandchildren. It was all completely mad and I knew it even as I spun the internal tales.

"Good for children," I repeated stupidly. In self-defense I changed the theme.

"Why this big flight from the city program?" I asked.

"How about Doctor Savio? He's left the city."

"For another city!"

Carla lay there, close to her own emotions, but a blank to me. In the early days of our marriage I'd hypnotized her, as I had so many girls in my single days, only to find that she was so perfect a subject that it threw me off my stride. She was a natural in some way I could not fathom. Perhaps I should try to hypnotize her into telling me—and herself— what was troubling her.

Instead I took her outside for a look at the moon. It had been full for three days longer than was thought possible by astronomers. The papers had been full of wonderment about it all week.

"Look," I said, pointing to the moon that refused to wane, "an impossible moon."

She smiled a white smile. "Remember the birds on our honeymoon?" she said.

"The ones that were lost . . ."

"Maybe the angle of the earth is tilting and we'll have to get used to new months, new shapes for the moon," Carla said.

"Or maybe birds and moons are changing their habits."

"Let's go inside. Where there's no moon."

But it followed us into the apartment in an egg-yolk-colored stream all the way to bed.

At that moment the thought of Crown came to me. I have no idea why. I did not know then that I would dream of him later that night or that the dream would pursue me back into my buried life. I thought of him only, at this instant, in connection with Carla. And I felt her malaise had to do with him—though, like myself, she hadn't seen him in years.

The thought was so troubling that I dropped the entire subject of Carla's feelings or my ethical drives and turned to furniture for the summer house, the Barton Bester account situation, my father-in-law's below-the-belt problems, his amateur anti-Semitism. Babies, moons, lost birds—all such themes seemed dangerous, heavy with meanings I was not equipped to handle. We made love again and she smiled into sleep. Unable to follow her there I was tempted to wake her up and tell her how I'd made light of the Bester account situation; how fearful I really was that Lester & French couldn't survive without it—that I would be called upon to destroy my job the next day or the day after that: an un-Rabbi with an un-job. Back where I was when I wandered into Lester's office and found my unexpected vocation.

Chapter 4. My position with Lester & French, that lively and perpetually ailing advertising agency, was literally a fluke. That is, I was a strange enough fish for me to believe that this was the only job anywhere in the world for me. Excluding such niceties as hauling lumber or digging ditches. I was totally unqualified for anything except the role of spoiled Rabbi. And Lester was the only tormented soul in the business world who could think he needed me to help him bring to bear the two-thousand-year-old Jewish ethical tradition on the real or imagined problems of the business that carried his name. If Lester & French collapsed or fired me and managed to survive, I would be beached—a forgotten, once-amusing footnote to a column in *Advertising Age* or a *New York Times Magazine* article on business ethics.

Perhaps I was afraid that if I woke Carla and told her, she would smile a sleepy California smile and murmur something about the Mafia being a myth—perhaps one of my ancient Hebrew myths. Some ironic, morally neutral, blond statement that would wipe me out and make my concern seem feverish, typically Jewish, overblown with anxiety. So I let her sleep and two days later she slept in the California sun. And I had only my Crown dream and Carla's discovered diary which I could not—or would not—read.

Carla was, after all, right about me. I was a professional moralist; my profession had crippled me as a private citizen. I was not allowed the slight excesses others were. The large ones were something else. I might possibly find justification for sleeping with another woman—(Rabbi Leo Wurtzburger of Frankfurt has written that there is no permanent protection against wandering affections). But secretly reading a wife's private thoughts: clearly unacceptable!

Many people consider that my job as Ethical Advisor to a large though shaky advertising agency is tantamount to being a special unofficial Rabbi to the business world. And, in truth, I never felt more rabbinical than when called into a meeting with several key account executives and Lester, the president of the agency, while they presented a case to me. Could one, with decency, handle both a beer and a soft-drink account? Was it permissible to advertise cigarettes at all? Should television advertising of a sexually provocative nature be scheduled late at night when small children are asleep? Such cases were, of course, the easy ones. But there were more subtle occasions. Barton Bester's restaurant chain was rumored to be controlled by the Mafia. Could we accept the account? A restaurant account would mesh so well with our food-manufacturing clients. But which was worse: to be allied with criminals or to possibly slander innocent persons by rumor? They would sit around the long Board Room table, suits and spirits buttoned up to their chins, and wait for me to decide on the spot, or to return to my book-littered office and search out some Chasidic text which spoke of rumor as worse than hatred, or in really elegant cases, something from Isaiah or the Book of Numbers which did not mention rumor at all, yet could be seen, when set in a certain light, to be an angry condemnation of hearsay. Or, on the reverse side, perhaps a quotation from Giordano Bruno to the effect that to do the business of criminal spirits when even the suspicion of guilt existed was to be worse than the criminals themselves, since they were following their nature in doing evil and thus might be forgiven more easily than the half-innocent accomplice.

In each case the facts would be presented by the executives concerned. Then Lester would turn his long, blue-shadowed face toward me. On it was the same expression that Jewish women had worn for centuries when presenting an eviscerated chicken for the Rabbi to approve or condemn. Never did I feel more ecclesiastical than at such moments. Even though I knew that half the time the account executives found ways to ignore or mitigate my more unpopular judgments. (I'm sure genuine Rabbis have the same problem of backsliding flocks. The heart is willing but the flesh is hungry.)

I'd first come to Lester & French for a job as a copy-writer. But when Lester read my résumé and saw that I was that noblest of all animals, an unpublished writer, and, in addition, was Jewish and had once racked up eight months at the Theological Seminary, he had one of the visions for which he is famous in the advertising tribe. I was thirty, and until that moment I'd been drifting from life to life. Music was gone, a casualty of some grass smears on a score; writing, a casualty of silence. With desperate gratitude I anchored in Lester's harbor. (A harbor that, in recent months, had grown increasingly unsafe.)

Now, ten years later, I was forty and having sound-dreams about Henry Crown and myself. It was time to see exactly who it was had slept in my bed last night. For a spot check I took a photograph I'd taken on my birthday twenty years before. I dug out the snapshot (O archaic term, heavy with memory) from an old candy box of my wife's; it smelled of perfume and dusty bobby pins.

Pasted on the bathroom mirror the photograph could be compared with my reflection: a topographical map of the years. It needed only the proper expert to interpret this bulge under the eyes as emblematic of some compromise, that set of lines near the corners of the mouth as the result of this or that character trait stifled or that or this sensibility destroyed by neglect. It was neither the map of a wanton —though plumpness always threatened—nor of an ascetic. It was the face, I thanked my destiny, of a man whose life was still in question. Or so I chose to believe as I began to wash and shave and scheme.

Chapter 5. I was ripe for some kind of personal plan. The sense of a painful and disturbing public life had been pressing in on me more and more for the last few months. It is difficult to tell if the private lives of myself and everyone I knew and many I did not know finally reached and poisoned the inner ear of government—or the other way around. It was different when I was young. Madness was a private province. Governments and other public fictions were quite sedate, rationally organized—with the exception of the occasional suicide of a senator or a member of the Cabinet (usually for personal reasons). This was just after the *Walpurgisnacht* in Europe in which governments and people had shared extremes in a democracy of lunacy. Perhaps it was in response to this that my generation expected—and received—public sanity and private dementia.

But in recent years politics had engaged in some kind of nervous breakdown. One year the entire City Council resigned. Then there were the incapacitating illnesses that struck only congressmen, then only governors, in a kind of random but sequential selection. (It was suspected that the hunger strikes which had spread to the United States from Europe via Canada—in spite of the heavy guards at all borders—might have spread to public officials, and this turned out to be the case but it was not related to the deaths in government.)

Then there were the months when so many young men returned all at once from the Civil Wars being fought in the chateaux of France and the cities of Italy. It was strange wandering the streets of an afternoon looking at these revolutionary veterans. It was naturally impossible to tell which of them had been captured and subjected to political castration. It was done at random, we were told, hostage-style. And there were, to date, over twenty thousand of them. So there was always a chance that the polite young fellow waiting on you at the stationery store, or the freckled youngster in front of you at the movies might have just a series of surgical stitches where his genitals had been. It made for an anxious fantasy-life.

It was in such images that the private and public worlds met: in the imagination of terror. And I relate them to sketch in the background of my personal uncertainties.

Late . . . must do something about it. . . . The words had an infinitely plastic quality. They now seemed to apply directly to me and my birthday. My private uncertainties merged with the public ones and all demanded one thing of me: a scheme. I had one; I'd had it since waking. The past was mine for the taking. All I had to do was stay away from metaphor and stick to reality.

Through breakfast I fed on my plan. Any insult takes two, I thought over the burnt English muffin. One to provide the occasion and one to accept it. A fortieth birthday was clearly an insult. Unacceptable!

The omens were good from the start. My father-in-law's health connived. He is eighty and has muscles I envy; but the prostate is not a muscle and if Carla's stated reason was genuine, the siege could last for days. I decided to discount any other possibility just to keep control. There was always a chance she would have gone along with the scheme no matter how mad it turned out to be. But if I was going to take the metaphorical "recapturing" of time and make it actual—well, such an enterprise was best acted out alone.

The weather, too, conspired. It was a Pastorale of a day. Someone had rubbed blue and yellow all over it. Traffic in and out of the city being suspended (for the last two days of every week—one of the desperate moves of the new mayor), I bicycled to the office. The streets were full of people on bicycles. It was vaguely festive; good birthday vibrations.

Chapter 6. INTO the density of the office, the murky fluoresence in which I daily swim. Here I practice my old borrowed formula: silence, exile, cunning. Only, to practice it in the heart of the business world, and without art—gratuitous noisy silence, crowded, pointless exile; and cunning aimed at survival for the sake of some mysterious, still-to-be-defined value—that was my pride.

This birthday morning, though, I was impatient. I could spare little attention for the mere available present—not with the enticing past waiting to be seized and held. But if the rest of the day was still ambered in mystery, the present, too, held its surprises.

In our deracinated lives surprises come most frequently in one of two forms: the telephone or the mail. Today it was the mail. I was summoned to jury duty in two weeks. And there was a letter from my ex-analyst's new wife informing me that since she was getting a divorce from Doctor Savio she would now like my help in getting a job in public relations. Clearly it was to be no ordinary day. On another occasion I might have pondered ironies, might have reviewed post-analytic feelings. But it was my fortieth birthday and action, not meditation, was called for. This was to be no imitation of Proust. If my plan worked, I would be new-born, even prenatal. Ontogeny recapitulates phylogeny! The fetus actually recovers every phase in the history of the species. So would I!

I bounced out of that office-womb and stumbled into Burns, the account executive.

"Hey, Walker," he said. "What's up?"

"Jury duty," I said. Fast thinking was the order of the day.

"Get off," he said, thinking faster, "Lester wants a review meeting—now." Thus I was hauled into my temple, the conference room: lined pads and pencils and charts my sacraments, the walls papered with subtle distinctions between truths and lies, over it all the fluorescent lights shedding their ambiguous yellow-white glow.

The clan gathered quickly. Ringer, the research man, Maximilian, the executive vice-president in charge of money, Burns, the account executive in charge of new business, and Scott and Werner, the wonder boys fresh out of business school, all graphs and profitability charts. Over it all Lester brooded, like some bony Cheshire cat in reverse: a disembodied scowl hanging in mid-air.

"Let's make it short," he said. "Jacqueline Frozen Foods let go fifty employees. Does that involve us, ethically, as their agency?"

"My quick guess is no," I said, over the muffled groan of impatience from several sources. "It wasn't our advice or by any action of ours. Just an economy squeeze. But I'll check some sources and be back with an answer tomorrow."

Lester looked as if tomorrow were an awfully long time to wait, but he moved on. Werner blew on his tinted glasses, wiped them, and looked through them at Lester as if trying to fathom that madness of the business meeting he was conducting. I sensed an undertone of suspense that, I knew, was the unstated question of the Bester restaurant account. No one would mention it until Lester did, and everyone was afraid he wouldn't—and perhaps even more afraid that he would.

"How about the Golden Lips product? Is your report ready, Wolf?"

"It's being typed. But the basic answer is negative."

"Why?" It was Maximilian, the money man, smelling loss.

"There's a peculiar ingredient the laboratory couldn't quite isolate."

"Which *you* pointed out to them."

"That's what I'm here for, Max," I said. Part of my role-playing was a kind of deliberate sententiousness. Rabbis grow used to manipulating the natural hostility of their flock.

Young Werner took up the battle. "There's no actual evidence that the stuff is damaging to the skin of the mouth, is there, Wolf?"

"Two women out of a hundred had bad reactions."

"Isn't that statistically negligible—in the area of absolute chance?"

"Where people are concerned we would like to be one hundred percent certain," Lester said. His position helped explain the slow growth and often shaky situation of Lester & French. To wait for one hundred percent clarity in any area was to wait forever. I would like to be, I thought, one hundred percent certain of the meaning of the words "Late . . . must do something . . ." But, unlike Lester, where people are concerned I would settle for fifty percent certainty, instead of the bewilderment I carried with me all morning. The air-conditioning in the conference room buzzed loudly enough to make me wonder how the spring day outside was progressing—how much sunlight bathing what stones on what streets along which I could pursue what shadows of earlier Wolfs. (If your name is Wolf, are your multiples referred to as Wolves?) There were two other Wolf Walkers in the telephone book. One was a doctor and the other was the director of some sort of institution. I assumed both were younger than I was. Sometimes, lying awake on disappointed nights, I would nurture the angry, irrational idea that one or the other of them—or perhaps both—were leading my life, on a second-chance basis. (My own special madness—or maybe the common madness that is at the bottom of a certain hatred the old feel for the young.)

At any rate, the lupine shadows of earlier Wolves were

waiting for me only as soon as I could duck out of present responsibilities. If I could hold off the questions about Barton Bester I could make it. Fancy-dancing and control of the agenda were essential. To the questionability of a client using a snake as a corporate symbol (sexual jitters from Lester) I counterposed the fact that one of the pre-Hittite tribes of ancient Israel used the snake as an emblem, innocent of any implication of Eve's temptation. I disposed of the question of an overly violent television show by pointing out that authorities differed as to the effect of such shows on the young.

Then, before anyone grasped my intention, I glanced at my watch, gathered up my few papers and made for the door with some mumbled remark about other duties. Scott was on top of me.

"How about the Bester chain. That's the biggest piece—"

"Research underway." I resorted to shorthand, in desperation. After all, damn it, it was my birthday. The child beneath the skin was growing petulant, demanding out.

Burns was an unwitting ally. He burst in with a question about a children's-toy account. They made war toys with soldiers who shed real (mock) blood and imitation bombs that actually (and harmlessly) burst before your eyes. There had been a great deal of discussion with religious groups as to whether they were pro or con war. It was complicated by the Church being against the chateau wars then going on in France, but not against the conflicts raging in Italy and South America since the resignation of the Pope. I thought it was all right for us to handle the account and had even convinced the uncertain Lester. But Burns had the confusion of the unmoored Catholic, thrown by the absence of a Pope.

"We have to think of the children," Burns said.

"Our tests show no harmful effects," I said.

"That's now. How about after they're grown up?"

"Oh God, Burns," Werner said. "Stop being a professional Catholic and let us take the million dollars' billing for the rest of the year."

"A million?" Scott murmured.

"Plus extra costs for creative."

"Listen," Lester said, straightening his perfectly straight tie, "I'm not going to careful us to death as an agency. Toys never killed anybody. We'll take the account."

I was just about safe. A few off-putting words about a male-cosmetics account that would conflict with our regular beauty products, and in any case had homosexual overtones, and I was practically on my way back to the past. The real subject seemed well-stifled and no one had the guts to raise it again.

Chapter 7. BUT Lester's magisterial office lay between me and the elevator. There was a door between the conference room and the office and Lester had used it to cut off my escape. He stood framed in the doorway. I usually thought of him as elegantly thin. Today he seemed fearfully gaunt. He was, of course, an intense worrier—only such a man would need an ethical advisor in the first place. A knife-sharp crease ran down his trousers; a taut handkerchief gleamed in his breast pocket. He was walking anxiety, a being held together only by concern.

"Good," he said. "I'm glad you took over the meeting." The word "glad" had no taste coming from those dry lips.

"How are you, Lester?"

"I have to talk to you."

"I'm in a rush."

"Rush some other time. I need you."

"The State needs me. Jury duty."

"Get off."

"That's what Burns just said. How would it look? The spiritual guide for Lester & French caught trying to evade his civic responsibilities." I was fighting for freedom to pursue my plan.

He cracked a leathery grin. "Remember the Eleventh Commandment: 'Thou shalt not get caught.'"

I followed him into his vast office. A plush chair enfolded me. Lester paced.

"I don't like it," he said.

"Like what?"

From somewhere a sheaf of papers appeared, clasped in his fingers. "This age profile of the organization."

"Have you had a study done of age?"

"It's eight point two points too old."

"Age isn't—"

"The older a man gets the more corrupt he gets."

"That's not always—"

"I want younger people. People who can bring humanism into business."

"How about Scott and Werner?"

"Those two!" He briskly rubbed the bluish beard no razor could cure. "They think we ought to take Bester Restaurants."

"Maybe we should."

"Have you decided?"

"I'm still investigating."

"I'd rather close these doors than take an account that was run by the Mafia."

"Lester, Lester, there's no question of closing doors." He was sweating in air cooled by more British Thermal Units than any office actually needed. "It's a question of getting as much information as we can and then acting."

"There's a lot of pressure on me to take it no matter what. It's twenty million dollars of billing." I watched him wipe his bony cheeks with an unspotted white handkerchief.

"And you're pressuring me the other way. You're a complicated man."

"Complicated—" Lester said. "It only seems that way, Wolf. It gets that way, but it started so simply it's embarrassing. Did I tell you that my father was in business?"

"No."

"A man who hated buying and selling. He would run into my room where I was studying—I say run in because it was always after or during a fight with my mother. It was always about the same thing: he wanted out of business and she could not see the way out. 'I have a new scheme,' he would tell me, leaning over my studying shoulders. 'I will buy high and sell low. The competition will be so confused they will flee before me as Goliath before David.' And he would laugh in his misery, an awful sound that laugh. He had a deep and secret theory that in the buying and selling process something basically dishonest happened. In that mysterious space between the making of an object for one price and the selling of it for a few cents higher—that strange sleight-of-hand called profit—something unnatural happened. He knew all the theories, Marx, Henry George. But my father was a visionary of capitalism, a poet of the profit system. 'Look,' he would say, 'If it were not basically wrong, why would so much dishonesty cling to it.' I was old enough and smart enough, by then, to point out that crimes had been done in so many names: reli-

· 25 ·

gion, government, family life. . . . And he would whisper to me in his mad, lucid way; '*They are all forms of buying and selling. We must eliminate every touch of the trading style in our lives. Then, perhaps, we can be happy.*' "

"But look, Wolf," Lester said to me as if I could see into his buried thoughts, "how can one lead a life entirely without buying and selling? The man was finally destroyed. He lost everything to a partner who knew exactly how he felt about things—and took advantage of that very set of feelings to do his dirty work. I was left holding the empty bag."

Lester's narrow, blue eyes were shot with pink at the rims —little skeletons of blood that haunted his appearance with a look of desperation. I felt a need to distract him.

"You're not your father," I said with a kind of stupid truth. "And these are more subtle days. Right and wrong are not written on the sky for everybody to see. The gods are invisible. And not just to businessmen. Silent, too. Everybody sells, everybody buys—who's to say how?"

Lester was not beyond a smile. When I'd first met him he'd smiled, big and robust, full of teeth. The present grimace was a ghost of better days. "That's why I have you, Wolf," he said. "You're not invisible. I can listen to you. Do you think I'm too extreme? Burns says I am."

"He may have a point, Lester," I said.

"My mother committed suicide. After my father's business went down the drain. I decided then that he had been right. I dropped out of the whole buying and selling scene. I wandered among Kansas wheat fields, Arizona dust storms—I bought and sold them. I traded day for night and bought it back again."

Impatient as I'd been, I was fascinated by this shadow side of my boss. "What happened?"

"I came back. There was no way out. But I came back

· 26 ·

knowing what my father taught me. You can't give an inch. If you knew the nights I spend going over the expense accounts, making sure they're all honest to the penny. But how can you? It would take a saint to control it all. There are some midnights when I think I'm going off the deep end, checking the last names of all the suppliers to make sure nobody's brother is on the take. But how about nephews? It's a nightmare." He sighed and blinked his bloodshot eyes like a man shaking off the effects of a long fever. "That's why this Bester thing is so important to me."

"I know."

"But you didn't know, Wolf. Now, you know. The account could straighten out the whole agency. But I can't touch it if there are crooks, gangsters, involved. It would be like spitting on my father's grave. It seems that I can't live without buying and selling. But I won't buy and sell with *them!*"

"Lester," I said, feeling his life, gray and airless, pressing in on me. "It's only business. That's all. Look at me." I faked a grin. "I got a letter from my analyst's wife today; they're busting up and she wants a job."

Eyebrows pushed up toward his scalp and Lester said, "Is she an analyst, too? I've been thinking, maybe we should have an analyst on staff. A really modern agency should be a full-service human unit equipped to handle all—"

My hand was a stop signal. "One visionary of capitalism was enough, Lester. Let's get a new account instead of a bigger payroll." (Trust a squashed artist to be the final realist while the businessman dreams.)

Lester made a pass at a reassuring smile; it was about as reassuring as watching a skeleton open and close its jawbone.

"Burns says you once knew Barton Bester?"

"We were musicians together; part-time Communists. You know, the good old days." Mentally I was slipping out of the office in two directions at once. Forward, I was mapping out the first locale for my Plan. I would go back to the apartment where Stacey and I had lived on Greenwich Avenue. God only knew who lived there now, but whoever did had better watch out. I was on my way back. I was remembering the Dance Concert for the Labor Temple in honor of opening a second front to help helpless Russia. Stacey and I were out in an icy winter twilight handing out flyers plugging the concert.

"Is Bester the kind of man you can level with?" Lester asked. But I was remembering the colors: white for snow, black for the beret Stacey wore and bright red for her hair brutally tucked under it. Through the dirty snow we performed our little radical ballet. Stacey danced to the right and then to the left, handing out a revolutionary patter along with the flyer. Less light on my feet, I missed my target more often than not. Actually, I danced with anxiety more than idealism or cold. The Village had hostile elements; Italian working people who hated Communists—the prospect of a left-wing modern dance recital was not a warming one to them. I trembled; Stacey had the courage of her innocence.

"Tell Bester what's involved," Lester was saying. "That we have to know the truth before we take his account."

The last flyer was gone, probably blowing into some back alley, when the crunch of packed snow underfoot became suddenly less friendly. Behind us I saw three enormous shadows. Without waiting to learn their shadowy intentions, I grabbed Stacey's hand and ran. Our shadows followed.

"Hey, Commie," one yelled.

"Commie-fag," another added.

If they were this personal from a distance, how intimate might they get if they caught up with us? I accelerated, whipping Stacey around corners, until the beret was lost and wild red hair gave our pursuers a flag to follow. Past startled tourists and, finally, through a labyrinth leading to our own (her) apartment, a labyrinth only Stacey and I knew, and into the apartment we fled, out of breath and amazed.

"There's your working people," I said, putting up water for tea to thaw our frozen bones.

"You don't know anything about them," Stacey said, loyal to her recently chosen class. The teapot whistled derision in that place of innocence and I hazarded a remark about the animus of the city. Perhaps the end-product bore no relation to the original clustering needs of people, no matter what their political needs. Perhaps no humanism could be supported in such concrete and plastic mazes.

"Humanism," Stacey murmured. "Jews are always talking about humanism. . . ." She had more stringent philosophies in mind beneath that rich head of hair, and later married an Armenian-American radical leader who was blinded and castrated in the battle of Chenonceaux.

I turned to reach for a pot-holder and Stacey bent to undo her splashed stockings. We collided, my arm with her mouth, and a red glob of blood on her lip testified to random violence in the city. So shocked was she—and I myself— that we ended by laughing, embracing, and crying, her blood pinking my clean white shirt.

"Well," Lester said, years later, "it's your job. I'm counting on you."

"Ah," I said, "perhaps you're asking too much. Man is not an adding machine—you can't count on him."

"Please don't joke," Lester said. "Try! Ask! Learn! Advise!

You must know how serious it is. I may have to cut the staff, drastically." The first hint of threat.

"I'll find out, Lester. Believe me."

"I'll have to cancel our lunch date today," he added. "I don't feel well enough to eat."

"I'm sorry," I called out, without regret, eager to escape backward again, to be off to invent a past for the present. It would be as difficult as writing, which I'd given up as hopelessly tough. First, to invent myself and then a locale. (The locale already suggested itself. Souvenirs of Stacey.)

"The immense and total memory," Henry Crown once quoted to me, "is a state of complete unity." It was from Benjamin Constant: the kind of writer he read. My memory is a sieve. But where the holes fall is rather interesting and often surprising. Example: I recall hearing a great deal about Stacey's later life, long after we broke up, but little of it remains. Except for the violent fate that struck. Memory escapes me as much as a sense of total unity has escaped my life. Splintered, fragmented, a crowd of powerful wishes and talents unorganized toward any central good, I pursue my way through Henry Crown's remembered quotations. (He spoke them as other men speak small talk.) And I pursued myself, now, rattling down Park Avenue in search of a taxi. First mistake! There are no cars or taxis. Besides, the subway was the proper transportation of the past. Token replaces remembered nickel. University Place replaces Park Avenue. Then crossing Washington Square Park a pockmarked Negro accosts me for some loose change. Crossing Sixth Avenue toward my old address on Downing Street the garbage lies uncollected in menacing heaps, the warm sun glinting on orange rinds and uncovered metal containers. Pastorales of the past would not be easy to create.

Chapter 8. IN front of the actual apartment, my impulse was to kick in the damned door. I am not a violent man by nature, but it seemed obscene for other people to be living between those same walls where Stacey and I had experienced the pleasures and the farewell scene I was planning on re-enacting. More likely, though, the feeling was an attempt to stiffen my determination. To impose on casual strangers any element of my past experience would have to be some kind of aggressive act—no matter how subtly or gently I tried to perform it. Will would be required. Instead of a kick I tried the doorbell. In the doorway stood a curly-haired young man, vaguely athletic-looking. Behind him my swift eyes looked for the familiar configurations of twenty years before. But everything was wrong. The phonograph was not at the window, the bar that had separated the kitchenette from the living room where my radical mistress had frequently tried to tempt me onto a floor or window-seat love only to end up in the middle-class bed (adumbration of my final future?) was gone. Nevertheless it was the right address, the right apartment, and twenty years later, to the day.

The young man shook my hand. "How are you?" he said. "I'm Jackson. It's a little awkward right now, but I'm glad you could come."

"Glad?" I said, following him into the tiny foyer.

"Well, to be fair, glad is something of an overstatement."

"Oh."

"But if it has to be done, and I personally think it does, then I'm glad to get it started."

"Listen," I said, trying to take charge of my experiment again, "my name is—"

At this Jackson whirled and called out: "Darling, he's here!" How nice to have one's presence, even one's lunacy, expected.

Darling appeared, blonde, disheveled, in a long red robe with eyes to match. "You can go to hell," she said. "I'm not leaving this city."

He turned old as I watched. "Darling," he said, the word curled with contempt, "this gentleman is here to see about buying the apartment."

"You're just afraid they're going to come and kill you. I'm not afraid. Why should I run away?"

He hit her and laid open her upper lip. A tiny spout of blood appeared as if by magic. That same blob of blood I had accidently produced for Stacey had reappeared, now clotted with intent—no longer random. What "they" could be coming to kill him? The morning was not beginning well.

"Listen," I said. "Lay off. That's not the scene I came here to play."

"You came to buy the apartment. What scene? What play?"

"Listen. I came to relive a scene in my life long before this place went co-op. I came to say goodbye to her—to Darling over there—because I was broke and she was restless and the revolution was still centuries away and—"

"You better get out of here, mister," Darling muttered through a wad of Kleenex. She was quite matter-of-fact. Unlike Stacey and myself, neither of them was apparently any stranger to blood. Jackson grabbed me by the arm. The word "listen" reappeared on my lips. It was, I realized, a flimsy weapon. I needed something more to control the violence that separated the past and the present.

· 32 ·

Chapter 9. DOWNSTAIRS I was amazed to find the day was still a beauty, though it was getting colder. I searched Sixth Avenue for a novelty shop and bought a toy gun, a plastic Mauser. It was small and neat and the next time I said "listen" someone would listen. But having taken that step I stood becalmed in sunlight outside the store, uncertain of where my steps and bicycle wheels should take me next. The street was strangely still. Two small boys sat on the curb taking turns in blowing up a yellow balloon. Each time one handed it to the other some air escaped and it looked as if the task would never be finished.

The brutal fact is, I was pushed backward into my life because I lost it so much more swiftly, easily, and completely than anyone else. I have always had a disastrous memory. It's not a memory, it's an illness, a moral failing, a tragic flaw; take your pick. The tapestry of my recollected life— which is really all we have—is full of enormous holes. I am no amnesiac; nothing so dramatic. The loss has been gradual, steady, and consistent. Of every age I've passed through I possess only a few days, or a few hours from those days, here and there. And, once I have them, they often vanish again, capricious as that element of time in which they have their real life. It is criminal, the pieces of my life I've let time and my vague memory steal from me. It's no wonder I couldn't be a genuine writer. I read somewhere of an occasion on which Henry James was invited to address a girls' school on the subject "How to Be a Writer." I believe he was wise enough not to show up, sending the young ladies, instead, a letter of literary advice. I recall only one sentence

from it: "Try to be one of those on whom nothing is lost."
Well, I am one of those on whom *everything* is lost!
Shade, detail, weather, specific colors, precise words uttered,
the whole contour of literal fact—all of it vanishes from
my mind and its powers of recall the instant life delivers
it into my experience. I'm always remembering something
utterly dramatic, all of a sudden. Such as the fact that when
I was in the Army (I remember that) a girl I was engaged
to and I got crabs, and we never learned who gave it to
whom and I was never able to convince her that I was
innocent of any unclean—or clean for that matter—phi-
landering. The engagement was broken! Dramatic? Comic,
too! Well I forgot about it entirely for twelve years. Only
after Doctor Savio left for England with his new wife
did I remember it. If Freud had not discovered the phe-
nomenon of repression, someone would have had to invent it
to explain me. And that's only one small example. My existence has always tended to escape me. Only by an enormous effort of will have I been able to recover any of it.
Thus, on this crucial birthday, my secret motive might have
been the fear of growing older without ever having had a
life at all, unless I could make some effort at holding it.
Along with the sense that I might soon be kicked out of my
present with Lester & French into a future so undefined it
seemed safer to go backward than forward.

Of course I remember being sick a great deal when I was
little—(how little?). And I recall my father's brother bringing me Howard Pyle's *Robin Hood*. But all I have of it is
the pockmarks on my uncle's face and the sadness of the last
scene when Robin Hood is being bled by some evil witch,
and Friar Tuck and Little John realize too late that he is
dying when they hear a weak and fading blast from Robin's
horn. Oh, I shall hear that cadence until I die. But is that

enough? Is that a life?

I thought, in the occult mood with which the day was filled, perhaps the part of my life that had been lived downtown was not ripe for reliving. It was depressing. People had been fleeing the city for so long now that whole blocks were boarded up. Real estate prices were low; one of Lester & French's accounts was a realtor and the impossible job was to write brilliant ads that would entice people back to the city. Even in the West Village young men were making evacuation plans and writing them in blood on their mistresses' mouths. And I walked away from that place where the idea of love and sensuality had gotten all mixed up with the idea of justice—ending twice in pointless, accidental blood.

Chapter 10.   I WALKED to the corner drug store where I bought a pack of cigarettes. I hardly recognized the brands any more. I'd forced myself to give up smoking as I had forced myself to give up writing. Both were self-destructive pleasures. But in my twenties I consumed two packs a day, and now I would like to have bought Twenty Grand or Avalons or my very first brand, Virginia Rounds. But I settled for choking a little on an unaccustomed Pall Mall.

Outside the drug store, near the lamp post, there was a hunger striker. He was camping on a pallet on which were piled all of his possessions: a few ragged books, pieces of clothing, a canteen for water, and—the hallmark of the hunger striker—deep-shadowed eyes, hollow out of all proportion to the curve of his lightly bearded cheeks.

It was such an extraordinary sight that I allowed myself to be distracted. I walked as close to him as I dared and said: "Are you—?" With a dreamy stretch of the lips he shook his head.

"I won't tell anyone," I said. "Are you?"

"No. I know it looks funny. Actually I'm a teacher."

"But still, here you are," I said.

He did not smile back at my smile. "Listen," I said, "what first gave you an idea to try this? I don't sit in judgment. I just would like to understand."

"I'm not doing what you think," he said, unable even to put the reality into words. "This all started with a small protest I was making because a student of mine was the victim of a political castration in Italy."

"And then—"

"It kind of got out of hand. These days you skip a meal and some government man is at the door asking questions. It's ridiculous. I have no intention"—he finally said it—"of starving myself to death. But just imagine—to be castrated at the age of twenty, filled with passion and the insane optimism of the age and then. . . . Something has to be done. Something . . ."

He hung his skinny skull on an upturned palm and stared vacantly at laked sunshine in a gutter-puddle. I envied him his suicidal fervor even as he denied it.

Actually, I was no stranger to the whole business, having met my first striker on my honeymoon.

Chapter 11. To make honeymoon expenses, I'd taken a travel-writing assignment. (My salary at Lester & French was adequate but not formidable.)

Honeymoons are, of course, merely a variety of travel;

one of the classic forms. We were to go to Madrid or Copenhagen. Instead we found ourselves in this magnificent fake chateau, all wide staircases and fountains seen through glass doors. The gracious men behind the service desk wore dark glasses: thugs who showed us to our automated, ornamented room and left us to our own devices. They were not many. Carla slept. I bathed and walked downstairs trying to brush remembrances of Paris, Glasgow and Verona from my mind.

The round courtyard was ringed with parked cars. Over them hovered the shaped trees for which this part of the Loire valley was famous. In the center of the circle a fountain surprised me with its listless fall of spray. A slender young woman was tossing something into the water with an air of expectation. It was pleasant to see. Our tour of the countryside had bogged down the day before. My assignment was to write a guide book about the wines and food of the countryside. But the hunger strikes that had been going on for some weeks all over the country had finally spread to the path of our travels. Naturally hunger strikes make it very touchy to get deeply involved in vintage wines and *filet mignon* with *sauce villandry*. I was not too disturbed. The assignment was only a pretext anyway, as was the trip. But it had troubled Carla into sadness. Such incidents as the railway porter humming the slow movement of a Beethoven quartet as he dragged our luggage from the train, or coming across an Italian newspaper in which the Pope was rumored to be on the verge of resigning—these no longer amused her. Only sleep and making love seemed to give her pleasure.

Coming closer to the fountain I saw that the young woman was throwing bread crumbs into the fountain. I circled her and then moved into the field of her vision so that she turned her head and half smiled. I say half because her eyes were so deeply shadowed that no smile could fully brighten them. A hunger striker, I wondered? Or just a tired tourist feeding the—the what? I could see nothing in the fountain except crashing water and in the stiller portions, shielded by a mossy statue of some fake nymph, whirlpools made by the plunk of bread crumbs.

"Are there fish?" I asked.

"Usually," she said.

"They don't seem to be interested in bread."

She laughed. "I think they're petrified."

And sure enough, bending over the water I saw, past the protecting shadow of the statue, two enormous goldfish, stiller than the water, hiding, fearful, in their gay, gold casings.

"You'd better find someplace where they're more grateful," I said. She threw a flurry of crumbs into the water and began to walk away, slender as a shadow. I thought that would be all when she turned her head and threw a crumb at me, over her shoulder. "No one's grateful," she said, and walked on toward the chateau.

To prevent myself from following her with my glance, I turned it upward—with an immediate reward: a bird with two tiny red crests between its ears and a white smear down its belly perched on the tree to the left of the fountain. It had just settled there, the branch still trembled. Unless I was mistaken it was an impossible bird—that is, it was a North American Double Crested Lapwing. *North American* you understand. In the Loire valley. I was delighted, I admit, because, frankly, I needed entertainment. It was not only Carla who was disturbed. Hunger strikes in twenty countries, after all! No one had as yet died; though a man in Malaga was reported to be in a very weak condition. It was an impossible situation in the worst sense. And here was an impossible situation in a marvelous sense. A bird that could not be here!

I raced up the steps of the great curving staircase to our room. Taking care not to wake Carla, I dug out the book on what birds cannot be found where, from my half-unpacked suitcase. Then I ran downstairs and panted at the foot of the tree. The Lapwing was still there, quite still, as if poised for my inspection. I checked every identifying mark against the picture in the book. The twin red crests, the white breast smear, the fanned-out tail. There was no doubt about it. It was a Double Crested Lapwing and it could not possibly be in France.

When I woke Carla up to tell her, she was sleepily impatient.

"How do you know?" she murmured.

"It's in the book."

"That book's a fake. I never believed it. How can there be a book on where birds *won't* be?"

"The picture checks out, absolutely. Isn't it terrific?"

"It can't be the bird you're talking about, because it can't be in France," Carla said.

"That's the whole point," I said. "That's why it's so terrific."

"It's not terrific if it's not true. It's probably a bird that looks like the Lap—whatever-it-is. Why did you wake me up?"

My darling Carla who had majored in Dreams at the University of California—and could not now believe in one lost or misplaced bird. I felt the excitement ebbing and abandoned my plan to take a picture of the bird, if it was still there. It wouldn't prove anything, even with the chateau in the background, if I could angle it so. There are probably fake chateaux in America, too. You can't prove anything to people who are determined not to believe.

In the middle of the night I was awakened by a scuffling sound at the window. I was actually half awake already, being natural prey to nighttime images induced by our tour: the *son et lumière* rituals we'd observed at the chateau the evening before, the lights flicking on and off, bats swooping down dangerously close to our hair; the images were running in my mind like the bats skittering on air; the rivalry between Diane de Poitiers and Catherine de Medici and the beautifully ordered formal gardens that were the result. I'd seen so much of order in our few days in the Loire valley, the inherited order of the kings and queens of France who had lived there, that the chaotic notion of hunger strikes seemed distant. Perhaps the birds in America were on a hunger strike and the Lapwing I'd seen was a rebel, come to the banks of the Loire for some *truite amandine* and a *demi-bouteille* of the local rosé.

I slipped out of bed hoping that the noise would not waken Carla. The casement windows were open to catch fugitive breezes. There, clinging by her fingers to the iron bars of the balcony, was the slender shadow of a girl who had been feeding the goldfish in the courtyard.

"Please . . ." she murmured. Quickly I knelt and grabbed one hand. Immediately the other one let go of the railing and dangled. Apparently she had been at the point of dropping off. I have no idea how she could have gotten there; whether she was climbing down or up, running away or toward. Carla was behind me. "Who is it?" she whispered.

"Get some help," I said. "I can't pull her up and I can't hold her for long."

While I waited for Carla, bracing myself against the window, I slowly slid down the glass until I was sitting on the balcony holding onto the girl's hand with both of mine. I began to babble anything I could think of, hoping to distract her from her situation—our situation—for I was, after all, now involved. "My arms are strong, don't worry. I used to play the cello in school." Her face was hidden from me in shadows, but what I'd said didn't sound too reassuring. "What made you—" I stopped that one quickly; it was not a good idea for her to talk; she might lose her hold entirely. If she was a striker it was hopeless; she wouldn't have the strength. She was strangely passive, an extension of my arms and hands, more silent than the French night. I began to feel my fingers cracking apart and my arms were ready to give way. I tried thinking of other things as when trying to hold off an orgasm. The girl was beginning to slip by the time Carla and the nighttime thugs in dark glasses arrived to save us both.

Carla and I lay in bed trying to comfort each other.

"Was she French?" Carla asked.

"I don't know," I said. "But then I can't even keep straight in my head how many cents to the franc and how many francs to the dollar."

"She didn't even say thank you."

"Maybe she doesn't believe in gratitude."

Carla was quiet.

"There are worse things to be doing," I said, "than traveling through France tasting wines and sampling local specialities."

"Yes," Carla said.

"I mean there's a man dying in Malaga."

"Yes," Carla said.

"And maybe I was meant for better than writing gourmet guide books—but maybe I was meant for worse. Do you remember the porter whistling a Beethoven quartet?"

"No."

She turned to me then with a dazzling smile.

"Maybe that bird is really a North American—what you said. Wouldn't that be fantastic?"

"It couldn't be," I said. "You can't go by books."

"But doesn't a whole species sometimes shift, change its home?"

It was too late for us to change positions. We made love anyway.

The next morning I opened the windows wide. The Loire valley shimmered in a mixture of sun and clouds like Maggie Teyte singing Debussy, like Monet paintings at the Metropolitan Museum on Sunday afternoons. The morning thug seemed more legitimate behind his dark glasses. Along with our two *cafés complets* was the Paris *Herald Tribune*. The man in Malaga was still alive but a hunger strike had broken out in Turkey; the first one in the Near East, and the rumors had been correct. The Pope had, in fact, resigned.

Chapter 12. Now, a year later, that strangest of honeymoons had the taste and tone of an idyll. There was little of hunger and quarreling in the memory. Gold-cased fish and lovemaking and irony, these remained: enough for an idyll.

The lesson was clear. I'd been too hasty in choosing my re-enactment scenes. It was bad enough the day had begun with my rejected Pastorale. Why, after all, choose a defeat, a difficult and painful farewell? Why not revive an idyll? A series of scenes unreeled, nervously, in my unclear memory. The reel stopped somewhere around my twenty-third birthday. The dark-haired Ellen with just the faintest touch of hair along her upper lip, who wrote passionate letters full of sensual detail. Remembrances of how we had handled each other's bodies in the enormous living room of her parents' Central Park West apartment, sprinkled with erudite quotes from the notebooks of Orlandus de Lassus and such. The memory having been achieved, I walked away from the violent Village, uptown, past Thirty-fourth street, toward a rendezvous with Ellen, the explosive young girl who could kiss or bite, depending on her unchartable moods. From her I learned the gentle cannibal arts of love.

She was a nipper, a chewer, a teeth-scratcher of flesh. She did everything short of drawing blood. There was in her some irritable inevitable association of passion with biting. In self-defense I began to force my softer oral activities into mouth-to-mouth-to-all-flesh warfare.

I remembered how I would take her home after a date and begin to consume her, beginning with an appetizer of plump, tasty earlobes, standing up in the long, dark foyer of her parents' mysterious apartment; until she was forced to allow me into the slightly less mysterious living room, where there were antique porcelain lamps, and a shawl-covered Steinway. I was Poor Russian Jewish and she was Rich German Jewish and we both knew that this, too, was a motivating force behind the furious, biting kisses on the neck and the intense squeezing of her breasts.

When I rang the bell I clutched at the fake gun in my pocket. I remembered, at that outlandish moment, that Doctor Savio, my analyst, the man who had the grace to smile through so many of my torments, real and fake, had just been divorced. Who would smile for him? And what would he say at my present experiment with the impossible? He would, undoubtedly, smile. The man had made a new psychiatric theory and technique based on the ambiguity of the human smile.

There was a girl behind the door. She could have been Ellen if the years between had been days: tall, gawky, with even a trace of black hair on the long upper lip. I felt like a poker player pulling ace after ace.

"What is it?" she asked.

"It'll take a minute to explain."

"Come in."

Chapter 13. WHAT trust! There was still hope for the past. I entered a paradigm of the musty bourgeois decor I remembered from a million musical homes of the Upper West Side. Walking through that foyer was like taking a guided tour through the debris of World War II: furniture as history. Doilies and elegant, worn Persian carpets are open textbooks. In the living room we were surrounded by the emblems of the successful refugee: the seven-foot Steinway, the overstuffed couch, the credenza filled with mementos of Italy and Spain, diploma from Leipzig, the cookbooks in five languages on the corner table next to the giant lamp, and the pince nez (with one lens missing).

"Well," she said, settling herself on the couch and tucking her skirt around her knees, "what is it?"

"What?"

"You said it would take some explaining."

"Oh."

"I have a few minutes until my next pupil comes. I live next-door and the Steins let me use their piano to give lessons."

Uncanny, again! Ellen had been a pianist and composer. I glanced at my watch—perhaps to reassure myself that present time was passing properly. It was almost noon. The office would be deserted except for the receptionists and a few secretaries brooding over sandwiches and aluminum foil. The restaurants would be buzzing with business talk and office politics and money. Burns would be discussing my abrupt departure with other account executives. In a California hospital my wife would be persuading her father to eat something more nourishing than the health foods on which he'd thrived for eighty years. But here on the Upper West Side of the past our concerns were with music lessons and sexual provocations and the uses of time.

After I explained the project to her she said immediately, as if afraid I might change my mind, "You can't stay late."

"Then kiss me now."

"All right. Are you going to fall in love with me?"

"Wrong tense."

"It won't do any good, you know."

"Come to bed with me?"

"With my parents in the house? Besides you're going on tour with that band—and I'll be left holding—"

"Holding what?"

"I'll meet you in front of Carnegie Hall."

"Twelve-tone is just a fad."

"Try this. It's more permanent."

"Quit that! They'll be home soon."

"It's been six months and I still love you."

"What's wrong with your eyes?"

"Conjunctivitis. But I was the only musician on the road who wasn't smoking Mary Jane."

"Square. I guess I do love you."

"But you don't want to do anything about it?"

"Just what I'm doing. Shall I stop?"

"Don't stop."

"I'm still quite young, don't forget. Young enough to be uncertain about you."

"Is that why you won't come near me? It was such a beautiful day at the Cloisters."

"You gave me your conjunctivitis."

"It's not catching."

"My doctor says everything is catching."

"Your breasts disturb me."

"They're supposed to." And then she added, trying to break out of it, "Wait . . ."

"No! Don't kill it!"

We were rolling on the carpet, dust in her eyes and my mouth. I found one of those troubling breasts and made my way toward it with a string of kisses.

"No!" She killed it by biting one of my searching fingers and was standing over me—still sprawled as I was under the piano. I sucked my copper-tasting blood.

"Wait!" she cried. "You can't just wipe me out. I have a life, too . . . and I'm in love with a married man who's bringing his child for a piano lesson—that's one of the ways we meet—" She began to weep, plump arms slicing the air. "How about me? You can't just go around manipulating people like some kind of Fascist. You're worse than him—turning it on and off, even in bed. I have dreams in which I get married but I can't recognize my husband's face. Terrible, cliché dreams of old Museum of Modern Art movies. All because of some impossible affair with . . ."

She looked enticing, blue blouse pulled out of the skirt hanging like a flag on a windless day, black hair sticking to sweaty spots on her forehead.

"What do they call you?" I asked, to push her off balance.

The irrelevance stopped her. She tottered, searching for an answer. "Lena," she said, finally.

"Look, Lena," I said. "What do you have in mind?"

"What—?"

"Yes, what? What were you doing waiting behind this door for me to ring that bell?"

"You're crazy."

She laughed a stagey laugh. Perhaps it was nervousness that made it sound false. "What was this girl Ellen like?" she asked.

"I don't remember."

"How did the affair end?"

"I've forgotten."

"Am I really like her?"

"I think so."

It was awful! A faulty memory is a kind of continuing suicide. Had everything been gradually fading from my mind, leaving only a bourgeois caricature of a daily lie? Doctor Savio had taken my past, collecting it in little segments, interlarding his collection with shards of dreams, leaving me free of its ridiculous compulsions. But should I be so *entirely* free of it? Should I not inherit it from myself? Who had more claim to it? All of it: the spider I killed at five and the one that frightened me at thirty-five. (Or was it the other way around?) The city boy excited by, and fearful of, the mute density of animals, the predatory insects, the searing sun. (When, at what age, and where?) The dream of being a writer. (But if I've given up writing, who is writing this?) The silent struggle with my father over money. All these banalities and their unavoidable distortions now belonged to Doctor Savio. And who, in the heat of the divorce, would get custody of it all? Perhaps it wasn't the excitement of recalling my Pastorale for Strings and Henry

Crown's baptismal destruction of it that set me off on my birthday search. Perhaps it was the sense of the poverty of my past. You can't hold the present, the future is a wraith; if you don't have the past you're really broke, tapped out.

Yet I swear I remember riding through a curtain of thin rain outside of Rome, on the way toward Naples; I skidded past trucks full of melons and pasta and kicked my brights just in time to shed a beam of light over a young girl on a bicycle, without a tail-light, and whom I would surely have crushed in another oblivious moment. And I remember I was only twenty-three then, and the vicious civil wars had not yet begun. And I remember the snow falling on my mother's grave before she was in it. Snow and rain and sun on a leaf-green park bench and teary farewells and a seven-course fish dinner at Sheepshead Bay the night before I left for the Army—devoured along with a girl who, untimely widowed, wrote me three months later that she was pregnant by me. (Three months!) And the first time I ever played string quartets and learned to play Mozart with just the right touch of heavy-hearted grace. There must be millions of such moments. You can fill in your own.

Thus, I forced myself and my memories to the edge; I allowed myself to remember the final, miserable details about Ellen: the lost and found prophylactic—that emblem of our old innocence—and a mother's outrage. Ellen weeping in my arms in a corner of Bickford's Cafeteria on Broadway and Forty-fourth Street, then departing for Cambridge—from which she'd graduated only two years before, and where she is, to my best knowledge, today. I was at a loss; so forlorn at this development in my brave experiment that it was a relief when the doorbell interrupted our defective charade. My eyes burned. A twenty-year-old case of conjunctivitis. But even that was less startling than finding

Henry Crown filling the doorway, eyebrows like bushes, face like a moon. The little boy with him was a small, oval version of his great, round father.

Chapter 14. CROWN kissed Lena and shook my hand in blithe acceptance of a random universe. "How are you? I see you've met Lena." His ironic eye watched her hastily stuffing blouse into skirt. My bitten finger oozed more blood, implacably.

"Her name is, for the moment, Ellen," I said, and proceeded to tell him what had happened up to this moment.

"Terrific idea," he said. "Only as always you've missed the real way to do it."

I ignored the dig. Lena guided the boy through the jungle of Scarlatti while Crown collaborated on my personal scenario.

"Don't just live," Crown said. "Rewrite." He stood marshaling all his fat grace, feet spread delicately apart, his pudgy forefinger pressing 20/200 eyeglasses clearer to his nose for a better look at me.

"Of course," he said excitedly, "why be so passive? Why do anything over again? Do it again—but differently!"

My sense of the ambitiousness of my enterprise faded at once. Before I realized what was happening, or who was in charge, we were off for one of Crown's classic Chinese dinners: Mandarin specialties with Jewish side dishes. Over Peking duck and sour cream and *dem sem* with *tszimmes* we traded reminiscences.

"Then I—"

"It was impossible to—"

"She couldn't—"

"There was too much—"

"Why didn't you—?"

"How could I—?"

We poured out the usual, colored by the fact of his insistence on endless marriages combined with brief affairs, by my belated wrestling with married life, by his flamboyant romance with the avant-garde and my tender relinquishing of the touch of art. Only Crown could bring back to me the bitter beauty of those days. (*Try to be one of those on whom nothing is lost.*)

Thorny, bristly days, days spent on the feet, somnambulistic, antiphonal with argument. Unsatisfiable days, stitched together with music and hunger. Long before I met Stacey I learned from Barton Bester and Henry Crown how tied together justice was to hunger and sensuality.

I was seventeen years old and starved for sex. With Crown the hungry state was the same, if the age differed by a year or two. Winter chapped our skin with snow as we trudged back and forth from rehearsals at Barton Bester's house. We were to perform the Brahms Clarinet Quintet on the radio. Barton sat whittling his reeds under the photographs of Karl Marx and Stalin which his father had brought with him when the Bester family escaped from genteel poverty in Hamburg to the life of a small manufacturer of children's clothing in Queens.

"The business cycle of capitalism is built into the system. There'll be another depression in five years," Barton said. His father beamed at him as proudly as a Rabbi listening to his pupil's Talmud recitation. When we began unraveling the complexities of the Brahms Quintet, Mr. Bester fell asleep. The revolution was in no hurry to arrive, he knew. And in the meantime, he had to manage a factory employing two hundred Puerto Rican girls. Barton had not slept with them all, but he was making progress. The latest progress was named Tessa and she had great slanted brown eyes. She carried Barton's clarinet case. In our starved state Crown and I could only gape enviously and make veiled references to which Barton would respond with amusement and—finally—generosity.

One strange spring night, all alien whispers of Brooklyn Heights, trees-river-and-streets, Barton's generosity flowered completely. He, Tessa, Crown, and I had been lolling on the grass looking out at the garbage scows on their way to their filthy missions. Whispers flew from Barton to Tessa. Crown grinned, and I felt an obscure thrill of sensual fear. Tessa's dark brown eyes seemed to look at Crown and myself in some kind of assessment.

"Barton plays pretty?" she said, to no one in particular. And as if she had said something hilarious she and Barton collapsed into shrieks and moans. Her breasts were shaking my control.

"Let's go to Tessa's place," Barton said. Crown took Tessa's arm and led the way. Barton fell into step with me, passing street lamps lending him periodic Mephistophelian guises as he smiled at me. "Listen," he said, "if you guys are hungry, there's no need to stay hungry." An elbow punched the point home to my ribs in case my mind failed to get and hold it. Barton, urbane as a clarinet, was making a profound statement. I was desperately silent. Tessa's perfume clung to me from the grass bed on which I'd inhaled it a few moments earlier.

"I mean, you know I don't believe in private property. I don't think Tessa's my property either." I stepped past obstacle courses of rusting bicycles and shadowy garbage cans as I tried to assimilate that subtle Besterian concept.

"You can't think what happens to a girl like that in my own father's factory. They get fifteen minutes for coffee."

I nodded in sympathy. "Some break," I said.

"That's how I met her," Barton said, transmuting injustice into sexuality with five small words. "Her family's Catholic, but she's not."

"What is she?" I asked. I was trying not to allow my thoughts to touch on the forbidden area: what was to happen when we got to Tessa's place. Where was her Catholic family? Were we all to make love to her under a giant crucifix? Rag-tags of tales and morals learned at the seminary ran through my brain, just out of reach. The entire lower half of my body seemed made of one big block of stone. I pushed it along toward Tessa's mysterious Catholic house.

"She's agnostic," Barton said. "Very sensual." He actually licked his lips, which were *his* most sensual feature, the rest being, in my young opinion, quite aristocratic, lean and elegant, especially when playing the clarinet.

Up ahead of us, Crown was singing a parody of the Brahms Quintet we had been mauling earlier that day, while Tessa giggled an accompaniment. Brooklyn Heights seemed, all at once, like some unglimpsed European capital —Rome perhaps—in the spring moonlight. My terror, however, was entirely adolescent American; my growing revulsion, entirely Jewish.

Barton grew suddenly volatile. He slammed one large fist against his open palm and said, "I hope when the people finally break out they *really* destroy it all. Everything!" He gestured ambiguously toward the unjustly treated Tessa. Then, without waiting for an answer, fury returned. He was in a wild state. "She's been hungry," he said. "I'm saying *hungry*, you know? I think"—he spaced his words for ultimate clarity and emphasis—"that-the-worst-thing-in-the-whole-world-is-hunger. I mean murder, all kinds of injustice, cruelty, none of this stands up to the horrible thing of being hungry."

I nodded, a million miles away and torn between planning my escape and trying to summon up some spiritual narcotic that would allow me to sink into Tessa's dark, inviting, formerly Catholic and now agnostic body. I was, indeed, hungry.

As if he'd guessed, Barton changed his style. Conspiratorial, the leer replacing outrage.

"There's all kinds of hunger. And, we're friends, so—"

I had, only that afternoon, been working out a musical aesthetic based on the alternating of surprise and inevitability. In music, harmony, melody and rhythm all defined themselves in terms of one or the other. In the midst of the good surprise there was a sense of inevitability (perceived a second after it happened) that colored it, and made it feel right. And in the middle of the inevitable there was a twinge of surprise that enriched it. I felt, in what was happening or about to happen with Crown, Barton, myself, and Tessa a kind of inevitable direction. I had been so passive in my hungers, allowing both of them to take the lead, musically and as friends, that the surprise of the situation seemed no surprise at all. But, with my usual habit of seeing ahead, around moral and ethical corners, I saw the inevitability of my pulling myself away from Tessa's flesh, felt my sense of remorse, of having been a ridiculous second. (Third, fourth?) Up ahead of me the moon shone on Tessa's hips, Crown's hand plumply appearing and disappearing around its curves. Damn it, I wanted more of the surprise and less of the inevitable! I was sorry Tessa had known real hunger and I was sorry for myself and my night sweats and fantasies of Tessa and her parts all magnified into monumental proportions, but my nerve was going fast.

"Look, Barton," I whispered. "You can't give—"

"She can give. I can share. Can you accept?"

"When does generosity become immoral?"

"When does being Jewish end and having balls begin?"

"Not so loud," I said. "I've been thinking about Laban and Rachel and Leah. Maybe there's some justification in that for this. What do you think?"

"You mean you need some document to let you—?"

"Try to understand."

"You going to do a paper on this for the seminary?"

"Be fair. I'm so horny I could screw the moon."

"The moon is right there in front of you. Don't be so stingy," he said, with a touch of subtlety I wasn't prepared for. "So stingy that you can't take. I understood her hunger and I understand yours." Saint Barton, feeder of the world.

We were at the corner now, where Brooklyn Heights changed its style, gave up all its middle-class pretensions and became an extension of San Juan. Houses grew stoops before my eyes, the women lounging on the steps all gained twenty or thirty pounds, and the men who murmured around them glinted gold when they laughed. Tessa's place —and my ordeal—were suddenly imminent.

Crown was at my side. "Okay," he whispered. "It's all set. I'll go first."

"Wait a minute," I said.

He looked at me steadily for a full strange minute. I could see one of his quotations to fit the occasion—in this case to make the occasion possible for me—coming to his lips. Finally it came out. "*All women,*" he said gravely, "*belong to all men, as long as there is a God to whom we all belong.*" He paused to let it sink home. Then, like a doctor who has administered the medicinal injection and seen it take effect, he grabbed my arm, ready to lead me to what I desperately wanted.

"Wait a minute," I said. "Where's that from?" Stalling action.

Over Crown's shoulder I saw Tessa fumbling in her pocketbook. The long curve of her leg, or at least the part uncovered by street shadow, seemed lyrically beautiful. As I pulled away from her she grew more desirable than ever.

"The Bible," Crown said. "Come on or she'll change her mind." Quick, inauthentic response.

"What part of the Bible?"

"Christ," Barton murmured, "I thought you guys were so hungry."

"I mean that's a strong idea," I said. "But if you made it up it's not the same thing."

"It's getting late," Crown said. "Okay, I made it up. I thought you needed a little moral and intellectual help. Now you're on your own."

Barton could see that, like all cowards, I suffered from an excess of imagination. "Everybody should belong to everybody," he said. "That's socialism."

"That's craziness," I said. "Besides, you're giving her— she's not sharing herself. I'm going home."

But I followed them meekly upstairs and only when the sounds from the bedroom became undeniable and, finally, climactic, did I force myself out of Tessa's dark, incense-filled apartment and into the streets.

Chapter 15. OVER the years I thought a good deal about the incident. I knew the classic interpretations: homosexual dread at meeting Crown or Barton inside Tessa's skin; or the more forgiving, but just as embarrassing, notion of myself as the self-denying Hebrew prophet (the twentieth-century version being, merely, the good boy.) The night before Carla left for California I thought of it again. It fitted perfectly into her sense of the crippling effects of the ethical style, the spontaneous animal action aborted by the moral considerations twenty times removed from the actual situation. Poor Tessa! What a weight for her to bear, after bearing Crown and Bester in the same night. What would have happened if I'd climbed on and slid into her accepting arms and mucuous membranes moistened by the sperm of my best friends? How would my later life have been different?

Yet, as Carla would have pointed out, that is precisely *not* the point. Those few moments, that night of my life would have been different. Guilty and ashamed or foolish afterward, but excited and passionate at the moment. Ah, that moon I was hungry enough to screw. Astronomers and astronauts cannot be moralists. My unexpected meeting with Crown brought back more than I wanted to remember.

"Listen," I said to Crown, as we walked the filthy streets that connected us to where we'd been before. "What did you really think about that piece of mine?"

Crown squinted at me from behind his milky spectacles. "What piece?" he said.

"That Pastorale I showed you in the park. You know . . ." (*Try to be one on whom nothing is lost.*) "Pastorale . . ." I sketched the scene for him; I was as eloquent as an impressionist painter, every rock gleamed in the sun, the grass trembled having caught the fervor of my need for Crown to approve my gifts and admit me to the sacred company of artists. Vaguely he tagged along.

"When was it?" he asked. "Before or after we all laid that girl, Tina?"

"Her name was Tessa—and we didn't *all!*"

"I remember," Crown said. "That was a good piece." Apparently, and surprisingly, he meant my Pastorale, not Tessa.

I was forced to describe to him in detail how he had destroyed my score and my ambitions with one gesture. His laughter shook all that roundness like a sudden storm attacking a whale. Wheezes underlined his amused contempt for my nurtured injustice.

"Oh, Jesus," he moaned. "All I did was throw you back onto yourself with a joke. 'If you're thrown on your own resources and hear a hollow sound, don't bother looking inside.' Lao-Tze."

"But you rubbed . . ." I was almost ready to laugh myself. Somehow this was no surprise. And my remembered sadness would do for a little birthday self-pity, but it clearly would not stand up under too much examination.

"Listen," Crown said, "don't lisen to anything Lena—I mean Ellen—says about me. You know women."

"Not too much," I confessed. "The only control I've ever had over them is by hypnotizing them."

Crown studied me as if I were a conventional but puzzling score, great gleaming glasses darting light-streams where the sun caught prisms. "That's right, I forgot," he said. "And you married that California girl with the uneven teeth."

Strange, the choices others make to characterize a woman. I would have picked a hundred other details, even different defects if that was what I was looking for. I'd never even noticed anything special about Carla's teeth. (Try to be one on whom nothing *important* is lost. I might modify James' advice. That rules out questions of teeth.)

"Yes," I said. "But I'm not too sure what's going on there. She's a little mysterious.

Crown shook his massive head. Hair flopped over myopic eyes. "Women aren't mysterious," he said. "Only secretive."

"Is that a quote?" I asked nervously.

"There's something missing in your plan," he said. "It's not ambitious enough."

"A new girl in my life always used to make me vomit," I said, determined, for some perverse reason, to demonstrate to Crown how little in control of important things I'd ever been. "My mother would wake up my father in the early hours when I'd come back from a date, retching in the bathroom. 'Pssssst,' she used to say, 'Wolf has a new girl.'"

Crown and I were kids again, suddenly jerking with coltish laughter.

"Do you know your Lena and my Ellen *bit* me?" A blob of blood still decorated the tip of my finger.

"What started this backward trip?" Crown asked. "Your child bride?"

"No. I'm forty today."

"So what? That's just an age. You have to be some age."

"That's form," I said. "I'm talking content."

"Ah." Crown waggled a finger at me and then propped up his eternally slipping glasses on the edge of his nose. "You want the raw material back."

"Doesn't everybody?"

"Not unless you feel it got away from you the first time."

"It always does."

"The hell it does. And I don't mean like that black girl of Bester's."

"Puerto Rican. Your memory is as bad as mine."

"My basic stuff doesn't get away from me. I've been trying to get away from *it*."

"Why?"

"Because it's hell. I've been living so close to the bone it hurts all the time." He gestured toward the girl who was whispering something to the solemn little boy. "She's just one—I'm involved with three. I can't let well enough go. I have to push everything past the next barrier. The raw material of love is woman, right? Well, I have to get more and more of it. That makes trouble—it makes torture. And the work: the raw material of art is your self and change. Those two together do it. So my self changes and the terms of the music have to change and that drowns you in change the way love and sex drown you in women. Raw material—shit! I wish I was basically a critical type like you. All you have to do is repeat and re-evaluate all the time. R. and R. R and R." He laughed and turned away from me in despair.

"Critical?" I asked.

"That Pastorale piece was a terrific example."

"You remember it," I said. Pride grasps anything it can get.

"Listen," he said, creasing his fat forehead at me, "I've just given up cigarettes."

"Good," I said, as if I'd been asked for a professional opinion.

"I mean have you got one on you?"

I dug one out for the apostate. He drew on it and surrounded us in smoke.

"Analyzing stuff is really your kind of thing . . ."

"How do you mean?"

"Lester & French, right?"

How did he know? Instantaneous paranoia; had Carla been in touch with him?

"Have you been following old friends' careers?" I asked—an attempt at fake insouciance.

"I read," he said. "Listen." (As a composer he seemed continually concerned with being heard.) "When you and I hung around in the Village, playing Brahms with Barton, hacking around the galleries, in the park reading each others' scores, or going to my folks' summer house in Rockaway, singing Bach canons in the ocean . . . or waiting for girls in front of the seminary . . . or going with that girl Stacey to rallies to save Russia . . ." (It all sprang into mind as he spoke, the special poisoned happiness of being young. Crown was a one-man cure for my crippled memory.)

"Yes," I said, eager to be cured.

"Did you ever, in your worst moments, think the world would turn out the way it has? The chateau wars were bad enough—then these nuts starving themselves everywhere—and castrated guys coming back from overseas—"

His enormous bulk drooped despair, his thumb dropped from its usual place securing glasses against eyeballs. "I remember looking out of the bathroom window when I came to visit you at the seminary; the view from one of the urinals was unbelievable, like a Corot—one of those big soft landscapes in the museum—all sloping green hills and smudgy grass. Then—I don't know what happened . . ."

Crown stared out silently, forbidden smoke swirling around him. He had created the past and bludgeoned it to death at the same time. I said nothing.

"Listen," Crown said. "Whatever happened to that great redhead?"

"Stacey?"

"Yes."

I began to track Stacey's fate down in the jungle of my memory. Something horrible trembled at the edge but would not move to the center.

"You know," I said to gain time, "I just went back to where she and I used to live. It was part of my overall plan. But—"

"Oh, shit," Crown said, savagely. The cigarette flipped past my ear and he seemed to regain the bulk and stature his depression had momentarily cost him. "Listen," he said. "Fuck nostalgia. Let me tell you what was wrong with that piece you wrote."

I nodded, afraid to speak. My dream of the night before had summoned Crown here to tell me. In a way, my experiment was already a success.

"You didn't understand anything about time. That's rock-bottom. If you don't understand time then you can't do anything with music. There's a poison that has to flow back and forth to the change of the material—notes, electronic sounds, temple gongs, taxi horns—it doesn't matter what the *stuff* is. But if you're not tracking those split-seconds right, moving the poison from one moment to another, killing little pieces of each one, killing and making worlds in split-seconds . . . if you can't do that, then all you can do is repeat what happened before, a little louder, slower, faster, or with different pitches. If you're afraid to use that poison—if you want to be so damned benign with your Pastorales, then don't get involved with music, or with art, at all.

"God, what do you think made me into a composer, anyway? Since I was a kid I've sat on the edge of time watching the moments go by, until I was blinded by a succession without content, time without substance, *abstract time*—there's nothing more scary; it's like death in the form of life. Early in the game I decided it was my mission to revive time, to fill it with the kind of thing that would bring it to life. To do that it's necessary, sometimes, to destroy parts of it. But then you can fill the rest with *real* time, changing, growing. You have to do what I've done. Isolate time from the world—make it into an independent reality, a solitary universe, an idea of eternity that replaces religion, even ethics (if you'll pardon me, Wolf); a strange process that cuts time off from everything but connects in new ways, that gets rid of the old conflict of protagonist and antagonist, makes it pure process. To make a density of time that absorbs the artist, the listener, the performer (that exquisite anachronism) and covers everything with a sensibility that's beyond being benign or cruel but which allows for infinite transformations and revisions. That's what interests me in your experiment—but you've got it wrong, the same way you had it all wrong in that Pastorale of yours."

Under this onslaught it took a magnificent effort of will, but I managed a word. "*Wrong?*"

"Sure! You're hung up on the same problem everybody else is."

Summoning another clever rejoinder, I said: "Problem . . . everybody else?" I was getting my wish and more.

"Form and content. Unless you fight your way out of that fake choice, you're finished. Once you get hold of the *shape* of your life you can switch the content any which way. Out of time or into it. But a dumb repetition is worse than just going on and on, birthday after birthday."

A yelp from the boy and an answering shriek from Ellen/Lena behind us interrupted my music lesson. Was she biting again? Crown ran back to see what was happening and I was left walking into a stream of sunlight so bright that the people walking toward me seemed only larger or smaller motes dancing and drifting in the sunshine. One of them slid along my line of vision and stopped in front of me. It was Doctor Savio, tall and white-haired in his wisdom.

Chapter 16. HE towered, dwarfing me in the shadow of his longitude much as Crown had broadly hulked over me. When the past impinges, it really *impinges.* Until Crown's appearance I'd had some feeling of the day's events being in my control. With Doctor Savio's arrival I had a swift sense of choice, things were about to slip out of my hands. I had only to deny Doctor Savio his entrance, his reality; in short, to re-exert some control over how and when my past life would be recaptured. I wasn't sure I wanted *it* to recapture *me.*

Perhaps it was time to straighten out the curve of the day and forget about the curve of my life. I could pursue the present task that I was carefully avoiding. Go and find Barton Bester, remind him of *auld lang syne* and receive the comforting or disquieting news that would be relayed to Lester. A simple job, accomplished by an easy drink together, a few laughs about Bester ending up in the restaurant business after being so concerned about the hunger of the masses as a young man. With that rapport it shouldn't be too hard to ask a man whether or not he'd sold his soul to the Mafia. At once the prospect of that unsayable sentence shook me so that I turned back to Doctor Savio in a delayed combination of pleasure, surprise, and relief.

"Wolf Walker," Doctor Savio said, "I was talking about you just this morning. To my wife." (Which morning of what month and year?) "I was remembering a dream of yours, trying to get it straight for a paper I'm delivering at the Society in London. (London, you deserter.) I'm going to compare it to a dream of an uneducated, untalented accountant I was treating last year. The contrast is fascinating—or, rather, the lack of it. Your dream—it's the one in which your family's summer home turns into the Garden of Eden, only the serpent is a kind of musical instrument and the colors— well, anyway, you know the one I mean . . ."

I had not the slightest remembrance of any such dream. But I would take it. Never turn down a dream.

"Well, this other fellow's dream—no, I can't tell it of course—professional ethics—but it was the most dramatic and colorful treatment of the Garden of Eden theme from the angle of his personal history. And he was a man without imagination, without style. I have no illusions about my patients after forty years of practice. Basic drives, problems, all define themselves pretty much in various molds. One sees every possible permutation after a while. But how about *dreams?* Dream material, that's nothing. Easy common ground. But, in their technique, that's the great mystery; not so much of psychology but of aesthetics." He threw me that shrewd glance that had seen me through so many difficult days. "How is it that an uneducated clod, as well as a sophisticated, trained sensibility, has available to it the complex, symbolic equipment of a superb poet; the landscape gifts of a Manet or a Magritte; mists of rain like a Renoir film; hard, cold sunlight like Flaubert; the language nuance of a Tolstoy; and the visual, verbal punning of a Shakespeare? Since dreams are only transmitted by a translator and never encountered in the original, it's hard to say if some people are greater dreamers than others—more original, more lyrical, wittier—more profound in the use they make of their materials: time shifts, colors, knowledge of characters, settings of scenes, transformations of wish to act (in more or less clever disguises). There are no aesthetic standards."

He was growing passionate, as Crown just had; his loose gray hair flopped around as he shook his head for emphasis. The past was full of people with serious things on their minds. Time did not seem to settle anything.

"But the same man," he went on, "who rises from his nighttime feast of images and themes often goes out into the world without the slightest idea as to the meaning of his experience. All right, that's explainable: repression, the pain of understanding one's self or the world too well. But what happens to all that magnificent resource of artistic technique? All that exquisite control of time, space, and implication? All those nocturnal Boccaccios and Raphaels? They wake up and lose their powers. Apollos serving in the households of the mortal, Admetus, they forget their godhood and are condemned to plod their way through another day. Apollos who get back their lyre only with the return of each night, and who must surrender it again each morning. It's a great pain to me as a psychiatrist. *I've made the discovery that all men are artists.* But I can't publish it because I can't prove it. Even worse, I've been skating on the thin ice of professional failure (my little metaphor, Walker). Even worse than that, unethical professional behavior (your little area, Walker). You of all people can easily appreciate the danger in seeing patients' problems, exemplified in their dreams, as an aesthetic spectacle overwhelming the medical aspect. I mean, there was a suicidal patient I had—a businessman. Unlike you, I make no ethical judgments—after all, we are all children of one Freud (my little joke, Walker). But this was clearly not a nice man. Cruel to his subordinates and crawling to his superiors. Still, he seemed intent on destroying his life. A medical problem. You might say the quintessential medical problem.

One day he told me a dream that was a superb vision of

the afterlife he was sure awaited him post-suicide. It was stunning, out of William Blake with images by Henri Rousseau. Where the brute soul of this man obtained such styles of vision I have no idea. (I remember one: a tree full of peacock's eyes under a sky that trembles sonically like the membrane of an ear.) But I found myself so struck by the beauty and inventiveness of the dream that I wandered up and down the paths of his paradise, fascinated, but not properly receiving the hidden signals he was sending. They were, of course, horrendously clear symbols of his suicidal intentions, even including the time, place, and manner of the act."

Doctor Savio sighed. He was either speaking quickly or my sense of time passing was getting heavier.

"He's dead now. It was a turning point for me. I realized that I was getting so deeply involved with the aesthetic spectacle of the dream that I was of no clinical help any more. It's all a matter of form and content. When we're *all* dead that may finally turn out to have been the only real question. Form: seductive, exciting, full of quick rewards—an affair. Or content: dull, yet elusive. In its explicitness always threatening banality, promising meaning but only rarely delivering it: marriage.

"Realizing this, I took my life into my hands, divorced, remarried, relocated in a foreign country—England, the language barrier (my small joke, Walker). My God, what didn't I do in reshaping the content of my life? I'm not quite comfortable with the form as yet; a wife who's a little spectacular for me to handle. Public Relations is her field (private relations used to be mine). And the new content has yet to fully reveal its meaning. But"—He shook his head, sadder than I'd seen him in three therapeutic years—"at least I've made a discovery. Even if it's a paradox and even if I can't prove it, since dreams are, like death, unphotographable. *All men are artists!* I've paid a price for that knowledge: no private practice, money hard to come by, my wife thinking of leaving me, going back to work." He touched his index finger to his nose in a manner reminiscent of Crown and said: "She said she might write you about it. Well—"

I leaped into the tiny breach, desperate to speak.

"She did," I said. "I got the letter this morning. Doctor Savio—" I said, and the air was suddenly brisk. Instead of a New York spring, perhaps a London autumn?

"Yes?" All patience.

"Listen," I began. Stupid of me since he had listened to me for years. But I was so deeply into *my* dreams I was beyond dreams.

"My wife is as foreign to me as London or a dream. I get hints of who or what she is, but only hints. She used to photograph wild animals. It's been a year and this morning I found a secret diary she keeps—"

"Women," Doctor Savio said, "are not simply secretive. They are genuinely mysterious. What was in the diary?"

"I only read the words 'too late . . . *must do something about it.*'"

"It has the rhythm," Doctor Savio said, "of a poem."

"Don't start that," I cried out. "You were my doctor for years. Tell me what it means. She's from California, a sun-creature. I don't understand her existence. And where does the ethical stop and everything else begin?"

"In dreams . . ." he began. "But I've forfeited the right to interpret." He began to move into lakes of the dazzling sunlight.

"*Too late,*" I called after him. "*Must do something.* It could mean anything."

". . . thing," I heard, and he was gone into the brilliance, and Crown's bellying shadow covered me and savage little Ellen/Lena and Crown's small boy.

Chapter 17.

I'VE got it," Crown said. He sucked a finger anxiously where Lena had probably bitten him, as she had bitten me—but for more personal reasons. When the finger came out of his mouth there was no blood. I felt oddly privileged.

"I've got it all set," he said.

Behind him the somber child giggled. The show, it seemed, was just starting.

"What do you have in mind?"

"Piatigorsky."

The name rang like thunder.

"I'd forgotten all about him," I said. But I was still stoned by Doctor Savio's dream play.

"This trick of yours . . ."

That jolted me. "No trick. Experiment!"

He brushed righteous irritation aside as he'd done earlier with sentimentality.

"Not ambitious enough," Crown said. "Let's find a real turning point. Not some dumb encounter with me in Central Park. Go back further, deeper. The whole question of being an artist or not."

Still innocent, I was the Candide of my time. Any old Doctor—Savio or Crown—could lead me. "Where, exactly?" I asked.

"Suppose Piatigorsky had accepted you? What then?"

It *had* been a key moment, just post-Army. My fearful mother and my tough but eternally unrealistic father had

· 68 ·

decided on a test. If the great giant of a Russian cellist would take me on as a pupil, I would continue in music. If not, science, sociology, business—every other discipline waited for me with outstretched claws. But I had been rejected by Piatigorsky, swiftly and surely. On such small decisions rise and fall the destinies of advertising agencies, friendships, marriages, lives.

I pointed out that to re-enact had been proving difficult enough; to reshape might be murderous. Crown agreed that some kind of convincer would be essential. At which I showed my ersatz firearm and we both roared with self-satisfied laughter. Lena produced a Band-aid for my bloody finger while Crown produced his Musician's Union Book which gave us the great Russian's address.

Chapter 18. WITH the fortuitousness found in dreams and occasionally in daily life, Piatigorsky answered the doorbell in the massive flesh. His bull's head was swathed in a yellow towel.

It would seem my past was the opposite of insubstantial; filled with people of great flesh and presence. My heart was pounding but Crown brazened his way in with a potpourri of fan-magazine praise and swiftly skewed his opening toward himself. Piatigorsky took the bait. We were all three of us well into the curving foyer, swathed in deep-pile rugs, by the time he found the breath or the presence of mind to say: "Ah, Crown, you are one of the maniacs who tries to kill music, is it? Gongs, graphs, pianos torn to pieces in bathtubs." His laugh was florid, blessed with grace notes.

"Be fair, Grischa," Crown said, with instant familiarity.

"Where were you when people were throwing rocks at Stravinsky for destroying music?" They had the easy rapport of natural enemies.

"Besides you mustn't antagonize me," Crown said smoothly, maneuvering us en masse toward the living room. "I'm working on a piece for Cello and Waterfall. I'll send it to you."

"Please, forgive me, I have a bitter headache," the old Russian said. "Just send the waterfall. I already have the cello." Delighted by his wit, he laughed again. At the end of the laugh, sensing just the right moment, Crown told him the purpose of our visit. I'm not sure what I expected him to do: call a mental hospital, or simply have us thrown out. But I was naive. He sobered immediately and, along with us, considered the pros and cons of what was to be done about my past. There was, apparently, no enterprise so mad, so childish, or so offensive to accepted logic that it could provoke rejection or ridicule. We have come to the point where no processes are sacred or free of question any more. Men may begin by dying and end up as infants. The cause will be confusion. Where there are no clear standards, everything is permitted.

"What piece did you play for your audition?" Piatigorsky asked me.

"The Dvořák Concerto."

"Difficult, difficult. . . ." He nodded. He was already in sympathy. This was going to be too easy. Lena watched, darkly, holding Crown's small son on her lap; they were watching a marionette show. Crown's plump fingers pulled the strings.

"And The Swan for pure tone," I added.

"Ah, Saint-Saëns, everybody thinks is banal. But to sus-

· 70 ·

tain is not so easy. Nobody knows. The tone . . ." He tightened the towel around his head.

"Yes, the tone."

"And you want all that, the playing of recitals, the tours, the names on the posters outside of concert halls, yes? And the love of the art, the grace of creating the phrase, the profound and witty musical line, is it? All the mysteries of art?"

I nodded and Crown grinned. What a coup!

Piatigorsky seemed to catch some of our excitement. He stood up. "You would study with me, then a management, and then the debut and the success, is it?" He towered over us. "We will assume the talent, yes?" I nodded again. One must assume some things in these matters.

Piatigorsky smiled: sunshine. Behind him, the actual sun and a great latticed window combined in a mottled sunburst borrowed from the flawless afternoon. The day was achieving a magnificent consistency. The plastic gun would not be needed. We could disband the victorious raiding party shortly. I rehearsed, briefly, the arrival time of Carla's plane, returning that evening from California. Already several small but urgent problems began to press. Should Carla and I buy a car if she were pregnant? On the other hand, was my sperm capable of producing life, since I'd never impregnated a woman, not accidentally or intentionally? Perhaps the child was not mine. If Barton Bester's restaurants were Mafia-controlled, why did not *one* of them serve Italian food? The questions of the present zoomed in on the assumption that victory over the past was imminent.

"Yes," Piatigorsky said. "I will do it."

None of us dared move. Then he turned his back and as swiftly turned again and thundered: "On one condition!" Crown started to say something but was silenced by the wave of a great paw. "On condition that you take those years away from *me*. Do you *know* what it is? Can you possibly *imagine*? One plays with fools, one plays *for* fools. Nothing one tries to do is understood. No! First let us go back to Moscow and dig up from the grave my dear Professor Nalistnicki. Let us beg him to change everything. To tell my mother I had the talent of a shoemaker; to implore her to send me into the Army, into anything but a life in art." He ripped the towel from his head and threw it on the floor. Where were his family, or servants, I wondered. How could we be sure that it was really Piatigorsky? There was no cello in the room. Perhaps we'd stumbled on some lunatic who was using us for his own madness.

"A life in art," he repeated. "A life in hell!"

He was rambling around the room now, an enraged animal, dangerous because his habits were strange to us. Mutterings: "Not enough your own torments in the work, but the idiot critics, the jealous amateurs. And how about these destroyers?" His finger struck toward Crown like a lance at a boil. "Centuries it took to develop a delicate instrument like the cello . . . from the primitive roughness of the viols to the gamba and then to the fine finesse of my Montagnana —an A-string that sings like a human voice. And what do they do?"—the finger punctured Crown again—"Electric sockets, tapes, amplifiers. The death of the ear, the death of the mind, the death of music. Add these killers—these— what is the name? Yes, the Crowns of this world, add their names to the list. Enough!" He leaped to my side. Grabbing me by the shoulders he jerked me up.

"You're right," he said. "My life is not a good piece. It needs revision. Of this you remind me. But how dare you remind me when you cannot help me."

I looked at Crown desperately. But he was already on his

feet and marching toward Piatigorsky. "Listen," he said, "this is not about you or me. This is about him." He was shaking with rage. "What do you think *I* could tell you about disappointment? When you try something new everybody thinks you're a fashionable whore. But it's not the newness. It's being yourself."

"Lies," Piatigorsky spat. "Whore! If you could write like the masters you would. You shock for the sensation. Whore!"

It looked as if the two giants were about to grapple: the circular struggling with the linear. But Lena joined the group and threw them both off for a moment. She was pouring tears out of red eyes.

"Whore!" she cried out. "My mother calls me a whore because I sleep with a married man. But a whore doesn't love. I'm in love and I can't stand it." She hurled herself against Crown. "To hell with all this past business. How about now?"

This last was almost lost in the sudden racket from the piano. Crown's boy was smashing his little fists against clusters of keys and yelling: "I don't want to play, don't make me play any more! No more lessons! I hate music! I hate you!" Piatigorsky was transfixed where he stood. Crown struggled with Lena who seemed to be trying to push him off balance and the boy kept pounding and shouting. It was a mixed-media piece for assorted lunatics.

Into this chaos there walked a wraith: a cadaverous young man, though, like a skeleton, he seemed to have no age. He was all cheekbones and shanks. His eyes were dim searchlights in deep holes. One by one as they caught sight of him, each person in the room stopped what they were doing. The last one was the little boy. With one last dissonant bang he delivered the silence in which, finally, Piatigorsky picked up the yellow towel from the floor and walked toward the visitor who turned and moved out into the long foyer. Piatigorsky followed him. One by one we trailed behind. The young man was gone and the great cellist stood, like a statue of himself, with empty eyes.

"Five months . . . ," he said. "Some days no food at all . . . some days no water . . . you read about it . . . but when it happens . . . and there is no why. Or too many whys." He carefully wrapped the towel around his lion's head, tied a knot and opened the front door. "Go," he said. "It seems I said no once years ago. I say it again. No! I will not teach you. You will not change your life. You will be what you are. I will be what I am. No!"

It may be that my nerves were so frazzled by this time that I was completely irrational; everyone's demands overshadowing mine, the second hunger striker that day. Or perhaps I felt I was being condemned to some perpetual exile I could not accept. I pulled the fake gun from my pocket and pointed it at Piatigorsky.

Chapter 19.   I HEARD Crown murmur "oh, boy!" Without taking a beat Piatigorsky summoned from his lungs an enormous bellow of wind shaped around the magical word: "*Police!*" I have had occasion to use the word and the call—once when I was in the Army on leave in New Orleans and had fallen into the hands of a petty thief, and once in Central Park when two men were mugging a pretty young thing. At neither time was there any response. But such was my luck this day that a few seconds after the cry flew out into the placid sunny day, two boys in blue showed up on the run, one of them fumbling at his side in a terrifying gesture I'd seen only in movies. Through the open door I fled once again into the city, running through the streets until it was either stop breathing or stop running. I don't know at what point I lost my blue pursuers; but I could not stop running, hiding for breath behind billboards, behind trash cans in demi-basements. It was an unguided tour of my city, a chest-paining, filthy blur that came to a temporary stop in an alley behind an empty lot on Broadway and Seventy-fourth Street. Sweat was in my eyes and blood was pouring through my brain. Breath was provisional and tricky; it had to be slipped past painful barriers in the chest, in gasps small enough to be acceptable.

There, surrounded by the junk-strewn filth and architectural elegance of the West Side, I sprawled.

Stitches chased one another through my chest, down to my sides and back again. I hadn't even enough energy to look around and see if Crown was hiding nearby or had taken his own trail to safety. Controlling my breath was almost beyond me. I conjured up the vision of Carla lying on the bedroom floor on a blanket of yellow hair practicing her Malayan Breathing Systems and tried to measure my intake of air. How the hell did she do it? Why hadn't I watched more closely instead of teasing her about it? Her teasing, in return, would use her father as a weapon.

"He can run a mile at the age of seventy," she boasted, "and have breath left over."

"Ah," I said, "but he uses that breath to attack the Jews."

"Everyone needs a hobby. Especially retired people. Hate keeps him young."

"All balls and breath your father, right?"

"Right," she said and then began to cry, struck down as she lay on the floor by the idea of the ballsy buck she'd known in her childhood becoming the prostate patient, the same lower areas in question, but the aggressor now transformed into a passive victim.

The memory gave me a moment to recover some breathing rhythm and I wiped caked sweat from my forehead and pushed hair out of my eyes.

A rancid smell of broiling steaks reminded me of my unfed state—it had been a long and foodless day—and of my avoided mission to Barton Bester. But how could I have been expected to behave responsibly when I'd almost pulled it off? It had been so close. Who would have dreamed the past and its Piatigorskys could be so accessible? I was, in part, terribly discouraged, but at the same time excited by the narrow escape from victory. The line between the Russian cellist's cooperation and rejection seemed so thin. Yes and No were closer than anyone imagined and some mysterious factors other than the ones usually blamed or credited were involved. Well, I had lost out on one gamble, one revision. But what could not be tried, if Crown's audacity worked?

A nauseous dizziness hit me, rising from the chest to the eyes and penetrating to the inner eyes behind the ones I'd closed. I was sitting in some kind of moistness; I dared not consider what kind too carefully. The sun winked at me from between two gray buildings decorated with the flying buttresses and fake balconies typical of the kind of apartment building in which rich German Jewish families like Ellen's lived and assured their children of piano lessons in return for respectability and grandchildren. Behind them, low in the sky, the sun cast a bright, cold light on my ambitions. No day could last forever, it reminded me. The sun was dropping and I'd been refused, chased, and Carla's plane was somewhere over Nebraska. *Late . . .*

A powerful smell of steak burning, fat sweetly smoking at

the edges of the rich cloud, tickled my nose. Ah, I thought, the tasty present. I'd lost Crown in my wild flight. But the police had lost both of us. And all I had left of my Ellen excursion was a stinging in the eyes and a blob of blood on my Band-aided finger. Voracious girl, she played the role of her predecessor too well. The years might at least have blunted her appetite for male flesh. People are so strange in their attitudes toward the mouth, what went into it and how it was used. My mother, a disappointed musician and a dark, gentle, moody soul—not unlike a female version of Lester—could not bear to pay large food bills. There was something guilt-producing about them. So, my father, a disappointed lawyer and an obliging man, arranged for the grocer to shift most of his bills to the dentist. And every month my mother would receive mammoth dental bills and pay them with a feeling of a deed well done. It was an early introduction for me to the relativity of ethical modes. But it was the wrong time to recall such matters; action was called for. Reflection could betray me to the police who could be anywhere in the vicinity. Having had little contact with them I had no idea how tenacious they would prove on a vague charge. (Vague? A threatening weapon? How could they know it was only a plastic threat?) I was wedged into a corner of the alley where I was invisible to all except some shrouded windows far above me. It seemed to be the back alley of a restaurant. As if to prove this, a fat gray cat sidled into the mouth of the alley. He (she?) had either grown fat on scraps or was pregnant, or both. My dizziness and nausea had turned to exhaustion. A wave of passivity took me. I would, I decided, if such a word is not too active for how I felt at that instant, follow the cat. Wherever it went, I would assume the road led to the present, where the past's police could not follow.

The way of the cat led only a few feet before it stopped.

The block was a door, a back door of some kind. Passivity was not to be the entire answer, I could see, because the animal was going nowhere, just rubbing its nose against the door and murmuring treble complaints to me or anyone who would listen. I was the only one and I opened the door and followed the cat inside. It was only a narrow hallway with a directory of tenants. I was not surprised that the combination of the recent events with Crown and the smell of sizzling steak produced the name that was third from the top: BESTER RESTAURANTS, EXECUTIVE OFFICES.

Chapter 20.   WHEN I was seventeen I'd developed a musical aesthetic I've mentioned before, based on the two poles of inevitability and surprise. No one, I'd felt, had come close to understanding the indivisibility of the two. You didn't go from one to the other: like *pianissimo* weaving a web of inevitabilities until a *fortissimo* surprise came in for purposes of contrast. All surprises, if they were valid, had to be felt as inevitable immediately. In other words, there are no true surprises. The sensation we identify as that of surprise is really the instantaneous attempt to deny the inevitability—followed by the equally instantaneous succumbing to it. It's no great jump from the surprises in the opening of the *Sacre du Printemps,* or the absence of them in the great G-Minor Fugue to the sight of that sign on the directory.

I had been sent out that morning by my boss to speak to Barton Bester and I was about to do just that. It was quite simple. The intervening events only furnished the denying emotion of surprise. But a destination has always been the place where you end up.

A two-line poem from that same seventeenth year (when I was making the crucial decision *not* to become a Rabbi):

Wolf! Is it a woman's voice that cries?
Why is everything we learn touched with false
surprise?

And, thinking about my surprise that morning when I'd discovered Carla's diary, I rose in the elevator, entered the anteroom of Barton Bester's offices and found Henry Crown lying on a couch fast asleep, looking like a beached whale. He'd found his way and, even less involved with surprise, had given way to exhaustion. His child and girl had been left behind in the hysteria of the moment. But Crown slept. That was the most clearly visible fact of all: Crown slept, belly rising, a gasping bellows, fish-like eyelids trembling over (it would seem) rolling eyeballs. His legs, half-curled under his great weight, twitched arhythmically. Crown slept as other people agitated; a running, jumping sleep in which who knew what Savio-like triumphs of imagery and style were being unreproducibly produced. He slept in a pearl-gray light like a self-created painting: Crown Asleep, Middle Twentieth Century. School of—

Chapter 21. "MAY I help?" A square, squat woman with a pencil in her hair emerged from behind a glass partition and came toward me.

"Barton Bester," I said, defensively. I had good reason to be defensive because the woman looked like Tessa, grown older and thicker. The legs were still supple though not as long as I'd remembered, and the mouth still glinted gold as she spoke, even without a smile.

"Do you have an appointment?"

Before I could gather the intelligence to answer, a thick man in a dark suit with a dark narrow tie joined us. He carried a walking stick and leaned cautiously on it, as if some recent infirmity or accident had made it part of his daily life.

"Do you have it with you?"

"What?"

"A wise look came over his blue-black cheeks and swollen eyes. "Does sleeping beauty have it?"

Tessa giggled, but strangely the yellow gleam was gone. Had the years brought dentistry as well as better and better jobs with Barton as his empire grew?

"Come on, Sperber," she said. "No jokes." Sperber stopped his laughter short. From behind a dusty window the sky darkened dramatically. The day's weather had been a shifting pattern of chiaroscuro, a series of Beethovenian contrasts, as if trying to compress a decade's weather into one afternoon. My watch had vanished from my wrist some hours before. Perhaps evening was setting in.

"What time is it?" I asked Sperber of the dark suit.

"It's time," Sperber said.

"Oh, Sperber—" Tessa said. But the jingling of a phone sent her scurrying back behind her glass cage.

"Okay," Sperber said. "Maybe you'll only give it to B.B."

"Who?" I said, determinedly thick to the last.

"Bester. B.B."

"Okay," I said. "I'll give it to him." When in Sperberland do as Sperber. That was my new motto.

Anyway, I was pleased at his name, having been braced for a slew of Italian names right out of the Sicilian brotherhood. Suddenly a stream of slim men in dark gray suits and dark narrow ties began to flow in and out of the waiting room, carrying papers and briefcases. They all seemed to be in their thirties and were very serious. Only Sperber, who seemed to have a supervisory function, allowed himself some edge of irony, a smile on his gray lips. He watched Tessa return from her phone call, smoothing her dark dress over her hips with a complicitous look that seemed to know we had shared some past moment.

"You look terrible," she said. "Worse than H.C."

"H.C.?" Everyone here seemed to embody sets of initials. She sniffed toward the couch.

"Oh," I said. "Crown. You know him. Does he come here a lot?"

Sperber laughed like sandpaper. "Mostly on payday."

"Do you want some coffee?" Tessa asked.

"Yes."

Her long, slow look followed the cup and saucer. Was she remembering? Or anticipating? She leaned over me as I sipped while she told me terrible stories about the intervening years. An uncle burned alive in a warehouse fire, an abortion in which the anesthetic hadn't worked. Sperber joined in with his tale of dropping out of college to support his family; a tour of duty in the Merchant Marine complete with venereal disease contracted in a Brazilian bordello. I was being drained by their confidences. I would have done anything to stop their flow. This Sperber's notion that I was there to deliver something reinforced my worst suspicions. Luckily, one of the gray ciphers passing by turned into Barton, looking only a little older, still slim and sensually elegant.

"Hello, Wolf," he said.

"Hello, Barton," I said.

We faced each other across the sleeping stomach of Henry Crown.

Chapter 22. "You're married, aren't you?"

"Yes. You?"

"Several times. Do you have kids?"

"No. You?"

"Several with each. You live in the city?"

"Yes. Country house, too. Small one."

Clearly, after years apart mere exchange of information was hopeless, and pointless. What was needed was not facts but accusations, probes, challenges, lies and counter-truths. We were beyond the detailed graphs by which people recognize each other and the way they live. Only our personal successes and failures balanced against each other could ransom friendship or at least induce recognition. Barton felt it, too.

"If you knew how many times I've thought about getting together," he said.

"You've been busy," I said, trying a light tone against the awkwardness of the moment. "Feeding the hungry."

"I've kept track of you," Barton said. "In my head at least." He pulled me past a series of doors into a vast room. It had none of the appearance of an office: long, comfortable-looking couches; low-slung chairs like saddles for weary riders, and one wall that held dozens of television screens.

Barton whirled on me as soon as I was inside. "Now that remark about feeding the hungry—that's why you've been on my mind."

"Why? It was just a poor joke."

He shook his aristocratic head. "It was a reproach. You're a spiritual advisor to that big agency, aren't you?"

"Ethical."

"Same thing. But you can see I've kept an eye on you." A phone peeped an almost inaudible sound but Barton heard and reached for it at once. "No calls," he said. "Except for Operation Story. I'm with an old friend."

He turned back to me. Long fingers shining with polish intertwined with one another—nervous reptiles. "Everybody has somebody they answer to—in their head. Don't you have one?"

I nodded. "He's lying asleep in your waiting room."

For a moment I was tempted to reveal the content of my day to Barton. But I resisted. My truth was not the question now. The problem was how to get him to reveal his truth. Not knowing how, I let him take the lead for the moment.

"You're mine," Barton said.

"I beg your pardon."

"You're the one I answer to, secretly." He grinned a perfectly straight set of teeth at me. "I'm good at secrets," he said. "Not one of my wives ever knew. And none of my associates. Except Crown."

"Is he an associate?"

"On occasion."

"But why me, Barton? A self-appointed Rabbi with a foolish, small R."

"That could be why. You insist on judging. I insist on being judged. We haven't even had to meet for years to continue the process."

I'd never get a clearer opening than that; judging—judged—all I had to do was ask. The words were structuring themselves in my mind, then in my chest and were moving into my mouth when Barton sprang to the long wall and began to flip switches.

"Look," he said. "Look how I've kept you and Crown and

all of us in mind." The television set nearest me flowered with images. There was a snapshot of myself standing in front of the seminary, wearing a *yarmulke* and a black suit. This quickly dissolved to a picture of Barton, Crown, and myself, along with two other musicians carrying instrument cases—a violist and violinist whom, characteristically, I no longer remembered. All of us were staring solemnly at the camera with the stiffness of young musicians who had just played a concert and were tired and sweaty beneath their clothes. Then a photograph of Crown playing the piano in his parents' home, perhaps a Chopin piece from simpler times. And finally a picture of Barton and his father standing side by side, in Barton's hand a massive volume of *Das Kapital*.

I turned away. Barton snapped a switch and the screen went black. "What happened to all your dreams of the hungering masses?" I asked. "You said judge so I'll judge. What happened, Barton? I remember you and your father in your angry Brooklyn apartment praying, brooding, waiting to change hunger, to change everything."

He turned a strained smile at me, half-teeth, half-pulling parchment skin. But he could not sustain it. It turned abruptly into an unpleasant frown. "Don't give me that shit," he said in a low voice. "You know as much as I do what these years have been. You know that's all finished now. How many times have you heard someone say those magic words, 'that's all finished now'? One by one every belief in solutions has turned into those four words."

Back to the screens, a different series now. Switches on, and a mixed-media history review appeared; it was all jumbled. Hiroshima came after the first chateau war and the first political castrations preceded Auschwitz and immediately afterward came the moscow Trials. There must have been a computer involved; it seemed to me I could hear the whirring of tape drives and cameras clicked from motion pictures to stills to videotape. For poignancy (or was it simply beyond Barton's control as the day was rapidly getting beyond mine?) there were extra personal visual memoirs. Right after an old faded piece of film of Leon Trotsky in Mexico City predicting the future of the working-class movement there appeared a shot of Barton as a little boy, perhaps eight or nine, playing the clarinet with a sublime clarity of tone; it was the Brahms Clarinet Quintet, probably with Crown and myself in the accompanying quartet, and then an old, cracked film of myself playing with a dog. He had a charming brown and white snout but I don't recall ever having a dog. Still, film doesn't lie. So I assume Barton had access to my past as much or more than I did. It was sad. What had happened to that dog? What had happened to me? It was all accompanied by a live commentary spoken by Barton; the cumulative effect was one of despair. That was the intention and it worked. I guessed he had given this show many times before, it was too professional, too convincing. When all the screens went black again he turned to me. It must have been convincing to him, its author, because his eyes were hollow, his mouth had almost vanished into his face.

"Now you see," he said, *"that's all finished now."*

All I could say was, "Then what's left?"

He came alive again. His mouth reappeared and above it his eyes, which had gone quite gray, regained their color.

"Ah," he said. "After those four awful words comes one more word. But it's a secret one."

On that he pulled up a chair next to the communications wall and we looked at each other in assessment as old friends always must, independently of whether I understood my wife or whether he was controlled by the Mafia; of whether he was supporting Crown as an old and broke friend or whether I still had secret desires to lead a life in art (a life in hell?). Did either one of us have a secret word we'd learned over the years, a word that would justify or nullify the way we'd spent them and the way we might spend those left to us? It was a comfortable, de-escalating moment, full of the gray stillness of late afternoon air in big-city interiors. I felt it every day between four and five o'clock: nothing resolved yet but nothing quite lost either, and the rectifying possibilities of evening still waiting low on the horizon. Outside in the waiting room Crown slept and the gray men plied their trades. Inside Barton and I would wait for the word.

Chapter 23. "You know," I said, "I'm here because I followed a pregnant cat."

He shrugged. "Any sign will do," he said. "If this were Paris the street might be called 'The Street of the Pregnant Cat.' "

I murmured, "*La rue de la chatte enceinte.* Nice." We laughed easily and in the relaxation of the moment Barton casually flicked on a switch and on one of the screens a dining room appeared. "Look," Barton said. "Let me show you some of the things I've been up to . . . since you're going to be handling the account." I let this pass. The moment for the question had not presented itself. "This," he continued, "is what's left." He grinned. "What you called 'feeding the hungry.' But we're far beyond that. In today's marketplace you need gimmick after gimmick. Especially in food. You know how I started—with the Plucky Pardner Restaurants. Here: cowboy costumes at the door, hats for the ladies. Look at them clanking those silly spurs. And watch *him* tearing into that stuffed steerburger. But I give them more than just food." *Click. Click.* Two more screens opened up. Sauces streamed from pans, fluffy French bread was torn apart in soft assault, an austere Maître d' bowed guests in and out. "Watch this girl absolutely become French when she starts on the *boeuf Wellington.* I give her hundreds of years of culture at a bite . . . watch that elegant little backbone straighten up—she has quite good lines, actually— reminds me of a girl I laid in Athens—Greek food is too cold and greasy—but there's no fantasy I can't touch." *Click. Click.* More screens. A Japanese ambiance fills one screen, sizzling vegetables and exquisite *politesse.*

"The starving masses of Asia—ah, God, it's lucky my father died before all the betrayals. It's just as well you didn't write the books you wanted to, Wolf. I did an analysis once of all the best of modern books. I bought some down time on a computer and checked out the main theme they all had in common. You know what it turned out to be: hatred of civilization. The computer never lies. You can betray hopes just so many times and then people turn back to the basics. Like food." *Click. Click.* Smörgasbord. Leggy blondes making trip after trip. I was growing dizzy watching. Or was it my fatigue and earlier vertigo returning? I hadn't eaten. And here this insane food-fantasia; this horrendous joke Barton Bester was playing on himself, replacing his political passion for justice with this restaurant attack on starvation. Hunger became a metaphor and Barton himself and all these clicking screen images of people-stuffing bordered on the comic, on—I was crawling around the edges of a word . . . would it be *the* word Barton had promised or threatened? It couldn't be, because as I got closer and closer to it, it grew more and more horrible—comedy does not banish horror, it sharpens it. But it was not a word one used about oneself unless one was a madman or was ready to commit suicide. Dishes clanked; I could swear aromas sifted into the room from the multitude of screens. Tables were shifted, wines were decanted and sipped, great mountains of beef, tiny delicate fish were torn apart, while Barton paced up and down before his food-wall, eyes shifting from one to the other, carrying on his narration, his justification. Desserts were drowned in brandy, sweet and sour sauces spilled on tablecloths which were whisked away by the uniformed soldiers of Barton's armies.

Hatred of civilization—the computer never lies. My unborn books would have joined in the sentiment. How could they not have? Bester's defection alone could furnish me with that theme. It was not enough to invoke the horrors done in justice's name to justify this—I had the word— *parody*—of feeding the hungry. Particularly if the parody was an arm of the Mafia brotherhood. I was getting closer and closer to asking the question poor Lester had sent me here to ask. Out of my returning nausea I roused my wavering attention to catch what I thought I'd heard Barton say.

"—is the word, after all."

"What?" I said quickly.

"Parody. That's the secret word—no secret now."

Click. Click. Click. Click. All the screens went black at once. I stared at Barton more horrified and paralyzed with surprise than I had been in a day not without its surprises. How can a man live knowing he's become a parody of what he was? I stared at him so hard that it seemed to me the force of my intense gaze drove his flesh and bone back upon itself. His smooth cheeks seemed to crumple in upon themselves while his bones protruded through, his lips vanishing, again, in the general debris and his eyes became moist holes. He was, even in this state to which my moral attention had reduced him, able to speak. He continued without losing a beat, impassioned, happy in his sense of his discovery and its truth.

"That's it all right," he said. "Parody. Didn't you know that forty is only a parody of twenty? (By the way, happy birthday.) And didn't you know that communism is a parody of socialism? That Henry Crown is a parody of Beethoven? There are no new forms, no new developments: we are living in the last days of Our Lord of Parody. Christianity is a parody of Judaism, sexual freedom is a parody of love; we hypnotize ourselves into believing we're onto something new. Only first things are worth anything, and there are no more first things, only parodies. All of modern civilization is based on that fact. I'm not ashamed of *my* parody. (I can see it in your eyes, Wolf, that *you* are.) I'm part of the mainstream of my time. You can't beat that for security!"

I was so shaken by this that all I wanted to do was get out of there. The easiest way to do that was to ask the question. And, desperation endowing me with the guts, I started to say the impossible phrase. But others were even more urgent and I was interrupted first by a buzzer, then a phone call and finally a troupe of gray underlings accompanied by Crown. Barton excused himself to me saying that this was a new venture of his called Operation Story. A combination of business and fiction. Recovering my poise a little I commented that the combination was a daily one in my business. Barton laughed, I laughed, and the demonstration began. Enter a young girl with yellow hair down to her rounded behind and a ragged young man with a black beard.

"What's your story?" Bester asked.

"She's my sister, a dancer, and she was pushed in the train station, twisted her leg, her money was taken and all we need is three dollars to make up the carfare to New Rochelle."

Barton looked at me for approval or criticism. I fell into the spirit quickly. "Where were you when it happened?" I asked the boy.

"In the bathroom. I saw the guy running and I chased him but he got away."

Barton looked pleased. Several of the fellows in gray commented, suggested improvements. I relaxed a little. It was a business meeting, a familiar setting. Barton explained the plan. He was expanding into begging. After all, owning the restaurants, he could quietly allow the beggars their stay in front of his restaurant at certain times of certain days. But for his clientele, sophisticated and successful as they were, good stories were needed. Thus, literature was a raw material of the venture. His business was becoming a branch of fiction and literary criticism: with immediate failure for bad fiction (that is unbelievable tales) and immediate payoffs for good fiction (that is tales that were not only believable but touching as well.) Crown was to be a guide to the cultural events around town: the front of a concert hall or a theater opening could be as good a territory as a restaurant depending on certain nuances. Was a comedy the best softener for a touch or a serious play? Did tears or laughter smooth the way to gullibility and charity? Was a concert of contemporary music a good bet—or would that deliver after-concert prospects who were edgy and troubled after an evening of deciding whether or not they liked this or that electronic tape-mix or this or that series of accidents, culminating in a piece for Cello and Waterfall. ("Excuse me, sir, but I'm a music student and I saved up for weeks to come to this concert and I lost my wallet on the train and—") Here Crown could guide the story material, but the agency could help with appropriate market research and copy testing of various stories at different events, as well as for different Bester restaurants. It would be, Barton assured me, a fine account; not only millions in billing but full of prestige and unorthodox excitement for our creative staff: a merging of business and art.

Chapter 24. SOME sense of self-preservation made me beckon Barton off to the side, then through the door into the waiting room. It was empty, nothing more than a glass cage and a silent telephone and intercom. Crown followed us. He was strangely silent around Barton. There, with only the three of us present, I finally spoke my piece in the form of a question. My theories of surprise and inevitability were borne out nicely by the next few moments. I don't quite know what drama I expected to follow my words. At the very least, powerful denunciations of my suspicions, statements of innocence, or physical violence at the outrageous idea. What did happen was: Barton turned his hands outward in the gesture that has meant innocence or clean hands for centuries and proceeded to confirm the fact that Barton Bester Restaurants, Inc., was indeed backed by and controlled by the organization known as the Mafia. And as he continued with a measured rationale of his situation my surprise stayed surprise; no sense of inevitability violated my mind for an instant.

"What you have to understand is that the thing you call the Mafia is not simply the organization of Italian *padrones* you see in the movies. It's everywhere and everything. The Mafia is the reality principle. It exists wherever there's a question of power and survival. Everywhere."

Barton's big paw extended to my shoulder. "There's no way for you to know how much *you're* involved with the Mafia right now."

"No . . ." I said, not knowing quite what he meant or what I meant by denying it.

"I don't just mean your taxes, or police payoffs. Though that's part of it. I mean the interlocking system of involvements so deep that if you're in the world at all—you're in with the Mafia. Oh, some more and some less. But it may not be entirely up to you how much and when and where." He turned to Crown as if for confirmation. Crown nodded. But, I remembered, Crown was on the payroll. I felt a grab of sadness in that part of the stomach where real depression always gets me. For my bold experiment to have brought me back to two old friends and to find them in the middle of this!

"There's a positive side," Barton was saying. "It's in every country in the world. Socialist countries, too. It's the secret life's blood of all economies. It's the one thing that's not parody; it's the original form. Buying and selling was always a primitive kind of force; that's the Mafia. Everything else is parody. It's nothing new. The Mafia was there during the Renaissance and before. They handle everything. They always have, so they're good at it. And they have the extra threat of secret force that makes everything work so well.

Only somebody hooked on failure could be against the Mafia."

"They have it *all*, Wolf, not just my restaurants. It's only a question of how much progress they've made in how many areas at a given time. But they, basically, have it *all*." He was trying to be encouraging; coaxing a difficult child who would not learn. "The state treaty and the state political convention (you knew about those), but also the art galleries, the music schools, the bus lines, the armies . . . The stuff about drugs and kids with needles in their arms, that's one tiny unit, like gambling; the romantic part. So, if you've got a real question, ask it. But don't ask me am I with the Mafia. Like everyone else the answer is: yes. Actually, the involvement with us is very small," he added cheerily.

"I wouldn't have let you in on that stuff inside if I thought it would upset you to know, Wolf. Don't you dare judge me on this. You don't know enough to judge me." His manner changed; a note of passion entered his voice. "But if you do, use the best sources. Take your own sacred texts. *But I returned and considered all the oppressions that are done under the sun; and behold the tears of such as were oppressed and behold they had no comforter; and on the side of their oppressors there was power, but they had no comforter.*"

"The Devil quotes—" I said.

"But it's true and it was always true. *There is a righteous man that perishes in his righteousness and there is a wicked man who prolongeth his life in his wickedness. Therefore be not overmuch righteous . . .*"

"Shit!"

"Wait, Wolf," he said, "Here's the clincher." He drew himself up until he looked for a moment as knife-thin and elegantly aesthetic as he had when we were boys together. He was trying so hard. This must mean something to him— my judgment. Or was it simply that he needed a good agency and no respectable place would touch him. These were deep waters. But one thing was clear: Barton's mad belief that he could justify his life to an old friend. He gave me the "clincher" pronouncing it slowly, richly rolling each syllable.

"*And, moreover, I saw under the sun, in the place of justice, that wickedness was there; and in the place of righteousness that wickedness was there.* Think of that, Wolf. 5,000 B.C. It's everywhere and forever."

This time it was I who would have liked to have yelled for the police, or God, whoever would come first. Instead, I ran. I'd run from Piatigorsky in guilt, I ran now in righteousness. I burst through that door and down those steps practically breaking my neck on a ball of squalling fur I assume was a pregnant cat. (Perhaps now a formerly pregnant cat.) I ran, head up, breathing deep gusts of the darkened air. Behind me I heard no cries of pursuit; I assume Mafia and police may both chase and perhaps even for the same reason. But one does it with storm and fury and the other secret and quiet as cream.

Chapter 25. INSTEAD of shouts and whistles I heard a lumbering and wheezing that could only be Crown. He might have been running after me in friendly concern. Just because Barton said he was on the payroll didn't mean it was true. But if it was them, the gray men, then they were in chase because of what I'd seen and heard. I ran faster, turning corners like a berserk motorcyclist without a bike. Stumbling and falling time after time, I tore my trouser leg on a rusty iron fence and found I was downtown, below the East Village. I slowed down for a second and then stopped. Behind me I heard the clumping and wheezing. Together we made the last lap and collapsed into the protective surroundings of what seemed to be an automobile graveyard. Rusting shapes of metal, fenders like giant shrapnel fragments lay up-ended in the dirt. Steering-wheel columns cast skinny shadows on half-opened iron doors, paint rotting away from their surface in giant rust flakes. Crawling behind the extended tailfins of a '43 Buick I found another hulk: Crown. I slumped next to him and managed to say, "Are they gone?"

"No."

"Do you hear them?"

"No."

Only the wind clumping old metal against old metal.

"Then how do you know we didn't lose them?"

He ignored this and rose on one elbow and turned the moon of his flushed face at me. The eyes, violet in the fading light, stared at me as if any moment they would see right into my soul and tell me what to do about it. But he blinked those eyes and he murmured, "Wish I had a cigarette . . ." and lapsed into another violent exhausted sleep. I lay back on the gravelly ground thinking of what had happened in the last few hours. I refused to swallow the Gospel according to St. Barton. *That's all finished now.* All hope dying in parody! I closed my eyes and felt myself shrinking into Lester's scrawny skin. I was more like him than I wanted to admit. And his father was right. Once you started buying and selling you were involved with *them.* Could that girl in the office have been Tessa? There was a danger in seeing connections between everything in the past. It was tampering with it that was dangerous. The truth of any past is a fiction one has agreed to believe. But what if all one's beliefs about that fictional past could be reduced to parody by time? Like Barton's hatred of the injustice of hunger ending in credit-card gluttony, and an elite corps of fictioneering beggars. And that speech out of Ecclesiastes! The power of the wicked!

Well, it would free me. I would tell Lester, the account would be rejected and I would be fired or the agency would fail or somehow or other things would change because of it. I turned my head downward until if I opened my hungry mouth I would have tasted dirt. I was the closest to weeping I'd been in years.

Like so many people of my intellectual class I had been troubled by the breakdown of confidence in public life. Hunger strikes, political castrations—all could be explained by the Bester theory. *They* owned the public world. All that was left to us was what the newspapers called the Private Sector. They meant the business world, but I meant the imagination.

Perhaps the Mafia could be transformed from being our masters to our slaves. What freedom for the rest of us, I thought in misery. Once the outside world is handed over to *them*, the inner life is free. And what freedom! A world without the pretense of ethical advisors, without ethics. Let the private life be determined by the impulse of the day, the reach of the moment. To be free of that clutch at the gizzard and the guts at the idea of right and wrong, that moral sensuality. To live in the present with my California wife and her wide-open, all-seeing eyes, but seeing only what is directly in front of them, turning the head only when the wider vision is desired, or when the yellow squint of the sun is too strong to bear.

All of which is to say: let there be an end to Jews. (*You Jews are always talking about humanism*—Stacey, 1953. *Jews are so—so good!*—Carla, two nights ago.) Let Barton Bester feed the world without my help. Carla and I could feed on each other and perhaps even feed a child.

Late . . . must do something about it. Maybe Carla had meant me and my life. Those six words were the key to my day's activities. Paranoia mixed exquisitely with self-pity. Ah, she would come home to a different man than she'd left. Would her mysteries yield then? Or would I stop wondering? Broke again, jobless again, dropped by the one agency in the world that would have me; all because of dangerous restaurants and beggars telling strange fictions. I mixed in some anger for color. And Crown, that son-of-a-bitch, with his Piatigorsky ideas and his ambiguous dates with Carla and his discourse on time, probably all stolen; what was quotation after all but stealing ideas, and all designed to put me in my place, but who the fuck was he to put me in any place, even if I might be grateful to him for locating what I was searching for?

I turned to the snoring behemoth at my side, his glasses held for safety in a pudgy hand, and poked him. He woke immediately as if ready to deny that he had fallen asleep, placed his glasses on his nose and stared at me. I took the initiative.

"What was all that stuff you were saying before about my music?"

" 'Time is linear space. Music is spatial time.' Cocteau."

"Don't give me that shit. I'm talking about my life."

" 'Experiment is a Jewish vocation. Gentiles accept the unfortunate nature of the world as the given.' Max Weber."

"I'm not saying I won't end up tomorrow morning just the way I was two days ago, except maybe without a job. I don't have any illusions. But this whole day will be worth it if I can find out something about myself."

" 'The Greek phrase "Know thyself" is simply a confession of the truth that others are too mysterious to understand.' Oscar Wilde."

There comes a moment in any enterprise when the sense of humor vanishes. It is the only genuinely dangerous point in human contact, and I was at that point now. I had endured chases, surprises with and without a sense of inevitability, torn trousers, hunger for an entire day, insults from Piatigorsky, insults from Crown and a bite on the finger from his mistress, and I had been chased by the police and the Mafia and was lying in a filthy resting place for the carcasses of cars. And I had lost any sense of the irony of it all. All I'd set out to do was to recover my life; a simple and universal desire. Whether or not I'd invoked Crown's presence or he'd shown up by chance, he was pushing me too far. When a man finds himself lying in a junk heap, he can't answer for his actions.

All of this foregoing apologia is to explain the fact that I began, at that instant, to pound Crown on the face. He threw up his hands to protect his eyeglasses and kicked out at me, catching me first on the thigh and then in the groin. I jumped up and kicked back. My first kick hit him in the corner of the mouth. It pulled blood, not a quotation of blood, his very own. And I'm ashamed to admit I felt a wave of pleasure at the sight. Obviously this running around in the past changes your moral and ethical viewpoint at least temporarily. He was on his feet and dancing around me with a terrific lightness of foot for such a heavy man.

Chapter 26.   CROWN tottered a little but moved toward me swiftly. I swung to meet him with delight. I didn't pause to be afraid even though he was much bigger than I was. It felt so good to be breaking out of the web of ambiguities into a clear and simple action. Hit, be hit. Barton had said there were no original actions any more, only parodies. But he was wrong. Physical violence is the one form that never stales, as long as it is spontaneous as with Crown and myself, unlike wars and boxing matches.

My glee stopped with the first punch Crown landed. It rocked my head and threw a bitter taste into my mouth, which may have been the beginnings of vomit, and I went down, dizzily turning and landing with Crown on top of me, his hands on my throat. I started to yell something, I didn't know what, and he squeezed his hands just tightly enough to stop me, but not tightly enough to choke me. Air whistled through my lips and into my lungs somehow, while Crown hissed at me:

"Listen," he said. "You and your fucking experiment. People like you are better off out of art. You can't handle it, you never could. You don't know when the hell you're well off— just live the way it comes along. That's all you're good for."

I didn't like what I was hearing and what I was going to hear if I lay there so I tried to lunge upward but I was pinned by Crown's mass, under fingers made powerful by years of percussive piano playing in the modern style.

"You heard Piatigorsky, you schmuck. You want a life in art? A life in hell, he said. You chose the right road for you a long time ago. Who the hell are you to try and go back on it? With all your talmudic arguments you're not involved with doubt, just with holding off the chance of failure by keeping it all ambiguous." His half-moon mouth opened over me in a parody of a smile. I'd never seen a row of teeth from below. It was like looking up into a descending saw. "You know what you're interested in? Success! That's what the moral life is: success. Success is just feeling good about yourself and that's why you chose the ethical style. An artist *always* feels bad about himself, somewhere, even at the best moments. And every time he does his work, makes something where there was nothing before, spoils that nice clean emptiness, he knows in some way that he's doing a bad thing, something antisocial, something unproductive, dangerous. I don't mean producing pictures for art galleries to show or pieces for orchestras to play—that's all politics, spiritual Mafia. I mean being a madman, a lunatic of transformation, a man who doesn't know a damned thing, least of all what's right or wrong to do. To *do*—my God—what has an artist got to do with doing? That's just life. If that's what you want, all you have to do is get up in the morning."

I was still pinned by his weight and by his passion, but his hands had slipped from my neck to the ground on either side of my shoulders. I didn't move. Crown laughed and I could feel the vibrations down to my pinned thighs. "Hey, I'll tell you what you should go back to. Tessa! Come on, get Barton, find Tessa and let's line up. And when your turn comes, climb on and shag her even if she starts to scream (and she wouldn't), even if you feel like puking all over yourself and her. I'm telling you, Wolf, only Tessa can save you, if anybody can. Right afterward, you know how you'd feel? I'll tell you—you'd have the perfect emotion for the artist. You'd feel disappointed in yourself. Not the sneaky moral disappointment when you've done something wrong that can be fixed by deciding to do better or being sorry. The feeling of being disappointed in yourself not for what you did—*for what you are*. For Christ's sake"—he began to lift himself off of me in a gesture that spoke disgust and weariness—"the dumbest hunger striker is closer to an artist than you could ever be." He stood up and brushed a cloud of dust from his trousers. "That's why that Pastorale was no good. It was just a collection of moments trying to feel good about themselves. None of that poison moving from beat to beat that makes music—that makes anything—" He ran a hand through his wild hair and placed his spectacles on his nose, carefully, like the dazed victim of an accident who does not realize something drastic has happened to him. "Anything but living," he said. "That's all *you've* got. Take it!"

I was able to stand now.

"Wolf," Crown said more softly—the first hint of tenderness I'd heard from him that awful day. He hulked over me, a vast impingement on the airspace around me. I saw his nose flared with tiny broken veins at the flanges, myopic eyes staring above, plump, hammer-fingered hands fluttering at his disarrayed hair. He loomed over me like a vast ruin among the automotive ruins, a '42 Crown getting ready for a last spin around my block. "Wolf," he said, "even if you could go back grab the Pastorale and make it your Opus One, write the books, play Piatigorsky's concerts for him, would you really want to? Do you really want to be like us, like me—like Bester's beggars, trying to move people with something that isn't true, just to get their belief, their sympathy . . . and a little charity?"

He was blurry and out of shape by now—a force, not a figure—some embodiment of the dual nature of things wrapped up in fat and fury. He began to tremble, transformed into a special form of matter, a unique kind of proto-plasm that was infinitely expandable, infinitely aware of it-self. Above Crown clouds bunched up. The day was reminding me that it still had one weapon left: night.

The distorted shapes of automobiles surrounded Crown until, finally, I could not separate them from him and he was no longer there. I rested against the fender of an an-cient Chevy and concentrated on regaining ownership of my breath. There were worse things than being caught by police or Mafia. All this, I thought, just to discover that everyone rejected their lives. That was old banality, yet there was a new nuance. Beyond the cellist's tirade of self-pity, beyond Crown's self-confessed damnation and Lena/Ellen's complaints—beyond Bester's parodies—lay the bony face of the teacher on the street and the staring eyes of the boy in Piatigorsky's house. Too many people were saying too final a "no." I had leaped back into my past life with a certain joy. And at every turn there was another "no." *Late . . . Something must be done about it . . .*

Chapter 27. SUDDENLY all my experience, all my silly days, the ones I'd caught glimpses of on Barton Bester's television screens—barely recalled, barely differentiated from one another—seemed unbearably precious (that unre-called dog with the brown and white snout). The neurotics who lay on their analysts' couches everywhere, as I had on Doctor Savio's—in idiot insistence on their specialness—all of them were right! As I had been right. All of those trivial dumb days *had* been extraordinary. Every crazy loon of us *was* unique as he acted out the same banal, universal, common, repetitious nonsense. Where were those days, beyond the reach of my will and my fake gun? The day I was drafted—the day that had begun in a Third Avenue cafeteria full of the early morning dead, coffee and goodbyes with my mother and my father, formal with fear—and found I had the afternoon to kill before being deported to a khaki country. I ran back to see Stacey, a poor, doomed girl who'd been kind enough to sleep with me. I ran into the tenement on Second Street whistling an exuberant theme from the last Beethoven Quartet, and heard the answering phrase whistled back as she came down the stairs on some errand or other and I grabbed her and we walked in the garbaged streets of those days—while some part of her conspired in her own early death to be enacted only ten years later. How many of those days were there? The task was staggering. The voice of reason whispers: If everything was important then nothing was. But my voice whispers back, No! It is only my imperfect control over my imagination that prevents me from grasping the sense of each of those hundred billion moments—or at least the days in their styles and weathers—or at least the months in their general outlines of happiness or sadness—or at least the years in their sense of gain or loss, at least . . . at least . . .

Chapter 28.   THE day was hopelessly out of control now; I stood in the automobile graveyard, tons of twisted rusting metal all around, and saw behind the wheel of a pulverized 1951 Chrysler a startlingly white-haired man who turned out to be my father. Lighting up one of the cigars I send to Denver for his birthday pleasure, he said: "Forty! When I was forty I had my own business."

"And when you were forty-one?"

"Failed and started all over again. You have to work."

"I work."

"You don't look good. Pale green like a pear. Red cheeks like an apple is better. You work too hard."

"I have it easy, Pop, really. I make money just by thinking and talking."

The old man shook his head through the cloud of smoke. "You were never practical," he said. "Music, writing, who knew what . . . ? But cash isn't the whole story either. In this life you have to . . ."

I listened eagerly. I said: "What, Pop? You have to what?"

But he drove the wreck of the Chrysler off and left me with a ruin of a '36 Ford convertible, the top torn into confetti and in the driver's seat another old man, his West Coast twin, my father-in-law, wearing a red vest.

"Wolf," he said. "What sort of a name is that for a man?"

"Tell me, Pop," I asked. (I don't know where I got the energy to curve a touch of irony around the word "Pop.") "Why do you hate Jews so?"

"Because you never leave us alone." He looked the way I'd always thought he would, gnarled and weathered, like an old rope from years in the California sun. "Do this," he said. "Don't do that. You and your goddam Tarah."

"Torah."

"Your Meshnah."

"Mishnah."

"Your Megillah."

"Gemorah. I didn't know my father-in-law was so learned."

"I had a friend out to Bakersfield when I was a boy. He went to the Yeshuva."

"Yeshiva."

"Yeah. Everytime I cheated on Carla's mother and I told him about it, he used to smile. A funny, put-me-down smile like he was Moses just down from Mount Synay."

"*Sinai!*"

"And now every time I get a pain in my prostate, like a punishment, I think of that shitty Jewish smile." He patted his bright red vest until it lay flat across his little pot of a stomach.

"But that's superstition, Pop," I said. And I could easily have poured out all kinds of rationale denying the connection of the prostate problems of age with the penis-activity, moral or immoral, of youth, all derived from the Torah, the Mishnah, or other such sources. But Crown had taken the heart out of me for such things. And, further, the thought of Doctor Savio restrained me. If I took the professional tone the result could be horror. If I took the aesthetic view it was comic.

But I was too drained to choose and in any case he was gone now, leaving me to walk through streets now filling up with cars, but not, it seemed, with a taxi for me. The bicycle on which I'd ridden out so bravely that morning was lost in the day's debris. I walked. At Thirty-fourth Street a woman hailed the only empty cab in sight and got in. She looked familiar and in desperation and fatigue I stuck my head in the window and said:

"Stacey?"

Chapter 29.   It was Stacey and we rode uptown in the growing dusk, and in the strained atmosphere that

surrounds lovers who are no longer quite sure why they parted or, worse still, why they had been together. Her Oriental-style high-boned cheeks and sallow skin had not changed. Madame Butterfly with flaming hair.

"Well," she said. "You look fine." She paused as if a question had been asked.

"And you?" I said.

"No, not too well."

"What's wrong?"

"The boy I was engaged to was in the civil war in France. He came back . . ."

"Came back?"

"You know what they do to them."

"Not all of them."

"One was enough."

"I'm sorry, Stacey."

"Yes . . . but tell me what's been happening to you."

I told her. She laughed at the right moments and was quiet at the others. The streets we drove through were a mass of cars and shadows as the sublime sun of the early day gave way to a fitful, low-key light, prey to bunching clouds.

I told her, too, how I'd been recalling our wild flight from the Italian super-patriots in the Village only that morning, during a business meeting with my boss.

"Is this the way you usually look on business days?" she asked.

I hadn't taken the time to notice, but my tie was torn from its customary place around my neck, the shirt beneath was filthy, my trousers were ripped, the Band-aid had come off my finger now crusty with blood. I had sweated and dried and sweated and dried and sweated again so many times during the flight from Piatigorsky's police and Bar-

ton's boys, and in my fight with Crown, that I was an alto-
gether unsavory piece of human flesh. The past was cer-
tainly a strenuous place to spend the day.

With the help of a handkerchief from Stacey, I repaired
some of the damage. The working day was almost over, but
there might be stragglers when I got back to the office,
working on the business I'd neglected. I had no wish to tell
her the reasons for my dishevelment. I settled for saying, "I
was thinking about you today. About the day I was drafted
and came back with that unexpected free afternoon and
found you on the staircase . . ."

"Whistling Beethoven back at you. Do you still play?"

"No, no more playing. When Piatigorsky said no, that was
it. You remembered the Beethoven," I said, pleased.

"I remember quite a lot," Stacey said. "It was the afternoon we walked in Central Park, even though it was Febru-
ary, and you hypnotized me."

"That's right!"

She laughed and intoned: "Listen only to the sound of my
voice." Her hand feather-touched my eyelids. "You are feeling sleepy, sleepy . . ."

Actually I was exhausted. I had to fight the urge to go
under.

"What a way to spend your last civilian day—hypnotizing
the girl you love."

"Were we still in love then?"

"We'd broken up a few times, but I think it was still on."

"Anyway, when you hypnotized me on the grass, it came
right back in a rush."

"And then that crazy letter of yours, three months later,
telling you were going to have my baby. *Three months!*"

"That's what being hypnotized can do for you," Stacey
said. She laughed, though she kept her face turned away

from me, and then asked: "Do you still put people under?"

"No. Not for a long time now, Stacey," I said. "Don't you sometimes feel as if all those years you were under some kind of hypnosis?"

She stopped gazing out of the window and looked at me, big eyes flooding with furious tears, her pretty, precisely even teeth chattering a little as she spoke. "Everybody feels that way about when they were young. But what kind of years have they given us since?" she whispered. "Half of the world is hungry and the other half on hunger strikes. And for myself—"

I wanted to say something that would calm her; something like "*they* don't give us years, we make our own," or other such homilies picked up at Doctor Savio's knee. But in the first place I wasn't sure that she was wrong and in the second place we'd reached Forty-sixth and Lexington and it was not until she dropped me off in front of my office building that I realized I had heard she'd been dead for a number of years: a suicide long after we'd finished with each other. Mademoiselle Butterfly, indeed; the most serious "no" of all. But there was, apparently, no stopping that sort of thing at this point.

Chapter 30.   I FACED the transparent building, all glass, whizzing elevators and tossed people. The newsstand vendor threw me a grin; girls' legs passed in unbusinesslike tumult. The sun hid behind a convenient financial tower. And in that shadow of hesitation all sorts of moments threw themselves at me as if it was their last chance. What a crowd! Infantile disappointments, outlines barely definable. Overheard remarks slippery with ambiguity. A nine-year-old chemistry set, a birthday present from my aunt, that turned water into wine as if there had never been a Jesus. A baseball game on Randall's Island when I was eleven, pitched by my father, after which I fainted in an excess of excitement and sun. The moment I knew I was going to marry my wife: a slow, poised moment, full of its own balance and gravity. A happy couple who'd lived next door who one day drove home a new baby from the hospital and crushed their two-year-old to death against the garage door.

To avoid being submerged in them, I stepped briskly toward the twirling doors, against the tide of end-of-the-day survivors. But there was a tremor in the air, some thrill of communication running from body to body; a shoving of tired, irritated flesh that was more than the ordinary rush-hour pressure. The pressure became a movement, the movement became a flood and the flood burst the restraints of normal behavior. A young boy, burly in his billowing sweater, shoved me against a bony girl who carried a suitcase. Her skinny frame gave and the three of us shifted down the street as if it were a stream and we were logs swirling roundabout in a jam. I almost tripped over the suitcase, stepped on it and was carried forward. A siren executed flourishes over the low roar of the afternoon. Its public shrillness was suddenly personal. After all, I had drawn a weapon against a man and run when he'd called the police. Sirens have blown for less.

But this afternoon they were clearly blowing for more. Three blocks of swaying bodies—one behind me and one ahead—were packed solid and moving in random thrusts and flows. I was already well past the entrance to my office. The mood of the crowd reached me now. I knew rush-hour crowds. I knew their sweats and their slouches, their rhythms. This was a different beast. Its fringe was full of neat-suited, attaché-cased office people; my siblings. But at the core were strange old women with stringy hair (the warty face of one was only inches from my eyes), and bull-chested workingmen and more cops than would normally be on Lexington Avenue at any one time. The cops were not in charge, either. Several of them were fighting their way forward; they, too, were trapped. The sun was as agitated as the rest of us. It sprayed the scene with light, vanished behind jumpy clouds, then appeared again. A short barrel of a man with a black mustache jabbed me in the ribs with his elbow. "I want to see," he hissed.

"See what?" I asked, but I spoke mainly to myself and he didn't hear me. I dug his elbow out of my chest, flattened myself against a building and felt behind me for a ledge on which to hoist myself. It was a double blessing. I was, for the moment, out of the press and I could see above the mass for a few blocks. On top of a parked car the gravitational center of the entire melee was visible. Two men crouched on either side of a seated figure. Even at this distance I could recognize one of the wraiths that had haunted the entire day. Slender as a pencil, unable to carve with his shape any substantial piece of space for the eye to catch onto, he was like a light lead scrawl against the sky. He looked vaguely familiar. Whoever he was, he was a prisoner and unpleasant things were being prepared for him. Motivated now, I shoved and pushed wildly until at the cost of much breath and a sticking pain in my side, I was only about twenty yards—or three hundred people—away.

"Kill him!" someone screamed.

"No, don't!" came an answering shout. But it was as full of hate as the first cry.

One of the two guardians on top of the car bent down

and caught something that had been thrown. It was a tomato. "Feed him that," somebody yelled, and the tomato was smashed against the prisoner's mouth. And then against that red gash were squashed what seemed to be eggs, cheeses, pulpy fruits, until his face was a filthy mess of edible colors. All this combining with the encouraging cries from the street made it seem as if the crowd had vomited over him. The last I saw, as several policemen reached the car and started to clamber up it, was a bottle being forced between his teeth. I foresaw broken teeth, lacerated gums and blood, and turned away.

Chapter 31. As I did I was knocked from my perch. Hands dragged me aside and my one clearly seeing eye showed me the blessed shape of a door. I had been pushed clear around the block and it was the rear door to my office building. The door revolved and I was inside; quiet and safe. I fled into an elevator and up to the fortieth floor. Whoever the poor bastard was, I thought, as I splashed water over the wreck of my face, he was neither the one on the street corner nor the face in Piatigorsky's hallway. I leaned my flushed cheek against the cold tile of the executive washroom and wondered at the extent of the insult. To refuse food was enough to shake up the world. Refuse food and you challenged the fundamental fantasies of everyone. Anything else could somehow be tolerated: strikes against war, strikes against any variety of injustice—and carried out by any means except one. Sit-down strikes, lie-down strikes, stay-awake strikes, go-to-sleep strikes, even suicide strikes. But strike against eating of food and you were in some area too basic to be endured.

I examined the evening face in the mirror and compared it with the morning face I'd appraised so anxiously, years ago it seemed. No change! Just fatigue, bluish stubble and some red streaks in the whites of the eyes. I'd done more harm to my face by staying up struggling with a rationale for a new client. Had the events of the day actually happened? I sucked the ragged edge of my finger-wound, proof of reality. What better proof than blood? Lena/Ellen had bitten me to stop our precipitous fall toward a past she wanted no part of. And my face was still the face of a man whose future was in question.

After the disorders of the day the office had a sweet sense of consequence about it. I wandered past the desks, row upon row deserted by their guardian secretaries, past the blue hum of the Xerox machine, the steel buzz of the electric water cooler. It was like a museum of a vanished way of life.

What was I going to do without it, my business-rabbinate? My doubting congregation leaning reluctantly on my faltering leadership? My safe haven of memos, of meetings, of decisions, which for all their momentary weight were only a form of buying and selling. I dreaded the next day's showdown with Lester. It would be a kind of death.

I turned the corner past the accounting department and saw that the elevator door was wide open—I remembered it shutting behind me with a comforting clink. Not only was it now open, I could see quite distinctly two hands extending over the metal doorsill. They vanished, reappeared and vanished again, accompanied by an awful groaning; a sound that indicated at once great effort and great despair. They were skinny hands; the knuckles were gnarled and jutted out from the fingers like knots in a length of string.

Chapter 32. It was hard to believe what I was seeing. Someone must have fallen down the elevator shaft and was somehow hanging on. I ran to the lip of the open shaft and knelt down. The figure I saw standing on top of the elevator car itself, arms stretched upward, resembled some kind of filthy, torn rag doll in mock prayer. It was Lester. And the instant after I realized who it was, I knew that, as I knelt to see, I had expected it to be him. Since that distant morning when he had canceled lunch with me and told me that sad tale of his father, the visionary poet of capitalism, it had been a possibility that Lester was to be—or already was—a hunger striker. For that was what his mad, pathetic situation told me he was. Even in the gloom of the shaft I could see his face was a filthy mess where the emissaries of the furious crowd had crushed food against his lips. Purple dominated; an odor of rotting eggs and something citrus whispered itself upward. My God, I thought, suppose someone rings for the elevator? He'll be crushed or he'll fall off and be caught between the walls and the car. I dropped to my knees and held out my arms. They did not quite reach his fingertips.

"Wolf," he moaned.

"What are you doing here? Never mind. Save your breath." I stretched my bones to the cracking point and our fingers touched. My face grazed a cold cable and I heard my jacket give way. An eerie interior wind blew up—or was it down?—in that dark and dangerous shaft.

In less than a moment Lester was hanging from my

hands. Looking down I could not make out his face. Only a year ago, on my honeymoon, I'd held onto that strange girl at the fake chateau wondering if she was a hunger striker. Even though I never found out, then it was a truth, in all its unexplainable fullness. Now, it had become parody: my middle-aged boss dangling from my hands, a hunted hunger striker.

Soon—I have no idea how soon—I was sitting next to Lester on the couch as he lay gasping and crying yet unable to stop talking.

"I had to hide . . ." he said.

"So you picked an elevator shaft."

"Best place . . ."

"Best place to get killed!"

"Happened so fast . . . One person points at you, another one stares . . . they all get the idea . . . you start to run . . ."

"That was your mistake."

"I was scared. They were so angry . . ."

"But why *you*, Lester?"

"Water, some water, please, Wolf."

After holding his head and forcing a few drops of water between those white, thin lips, I sat him up and tried to clean him off with the help of the remaining water and a handkerchief. While I returned some sense of order to his appearance, he carried on.

"I lied to you," he said, his voice like a hoarse flute. "It wasn't my father."

"Shhh," I said, as if to a child. I wiped a foul fleck of egg-white from the corner of his mouth.

"It was me," he went on. "Everybody says it's their father, whatever it is, but it's really them."

There were irregular streaks of blood above his upper lip.

A chipped tooth gleamed in the right corner of his jaw; it discouraged me from closer investigation. I helped him stand and tried to straighten his ripped shirt with its remaining shreds of a tie.

The two of us must have been some sight. Me, dirty and disheveled, with torn trousers and now a sleeve partially dangling from my jacket; Lester a totally pulverized wreck.

"And he didn't commit suicide," Lester said, resting his hands on my shoulders, whether for comforting contact or just to steady himself I did not know. "It was me. I just found myself so full of disgust that I couldn't eat. They have a name for it. *Anorexia nervosa,* my doctor calls it. But you and I know it was just plain disgust. If you're any good, Wolf, sooner or later it comes down to disgust. More and more people feel that way. That's why they got so mad downstairs."

"Yes," I said, trying to sound soothing.

I stared at the shrunken figure. I wished at that moment for Carla's eyes. Only her vision could, in its extraordinary clarity, give me the sense of what moral miseries were being expressed by this little mound of flesh that was receding even further beneath my gaze. Perhaps if I didn't listen to a word, if I totally abandoned the aural function, only looked, the truth of Lester's predicament might be revealed to me.

What I mean is that I felt myself being torn away from the message I would have to give him, sooner or later. I could, perhaps, put it in my own exhausted style: "Disgust justified . . . Mafia everywhere . . . Bester is Mafia . . ."

I finished the primitive ablutions which seemed to give Lester some suspected strength. He stood up as straight as he could, tugged at his shamble of a suit and said with some dignity: "Thank you, Wolf."

"You're welcome, Lester," I said soberly.

"Now—" he said.

"Yes?"

"Any word?" Crisis coming.

"Word?" Crisis stalled.

"On the Bester business." Crisis here!

"Oh." An awful blackness invaded my mind. My ears roared as if I were a child holding a sea shell up to the eardrum.

"Well?"

Chapter 33.   IT was, I imagine, the moment all my training had fitted me for. It was to make this reply that I had studied the Ethics of the Fathers at the age of six. It was for this that I'd built my careful structure of belief and authenticity. It was for this moment that I'd let Carla taunt me during our troubled midnights. It was this simple moment of reporting what I knew to be the truth and drawing the inferences of actions that follow for which my entire discipline had prepared me. It would seem to be, also, one of those rare moments when the truth came unwrapped in ambiguities, cool and clear as the water with which I'd bathed Lester's flushed forehead.

But in order to say the words I would have to shut my eyes. Because the words could kill him. How can you add one more iota of disgust to a man carrying such an immense load, not to mention helping him commit financial suicide and tempting him to moral compromise?

My eyes would not close and as I stared at his face it grew more and more skeletal. Cheekbones jutted out, eyes deserted sockets, hairline receded over bare-boned skull. I'd seen Barton in the same skull-and-bones style for an instant also. If you looked into the past, you seemed to get flashes of the far future as well. I could not say the words. If I told the truth it would be a parody. I said other words . . . "he's clean." The flesh returned to Lester's face, full mouth abandoning the rigid grimace. A hand reached up and touched my cheek. It was both sweaty and ice-cold. It moved across my face gratefully as if Lester was blind and could trace a Braille truth with his fingers.

"He is?" Lester said. "No connections?"

"None." I said.

"Thank God," he whispered. He reached down, removed his shoes and began to massage his toes briskly. It would seem that Lester was going to live. I fought the natural urge to give in to feeling disgust at myself for what I'd done. And in desperate defense I decided that my simple act joined me to the masters of history. All those who, faced with human pain, chose to lie. Children, presidents, doctors, generals: it was one of the threads that continued the tapestry of events unchanged since Abraham lied to God about his conviction that he could find just men in the city of Sodom.

The last temptation is the greatest treason:
To do the right deed for the wrong reason.

And what about the wrong deed for the right reason? That had been *my* temptation. I'd succumbed; and the feminine part of me, that is, the artist-part that Crown had scorned, took a certain pleasure in that yielding.

"Wolf . . ." Lester called after me as I began to sneak back to my office.

"Yes?"

"Don't forget to check out that age-profile tomorrow. We need more younger men. They'll keep us straight."

"And when they get older . . . ?" I asked, but did not wait to hear his answer.

Chapter 34.   In my corner office the mail lay neatly on the desk where I'd left it. Doctor Savio was still getting a divorce and his wife would still like a job in Public Relations—having apparently failed in Private Relations. And I was still being summoned to sit in judgment on some peer of mine who was being charged with fraud or theft or murder or perhaps just with the refusal to eat.

It's reached management, I thought. The professionally cheery sellers of goods and services will now be staring vacantly, despairingly, out of their fortieth-floor windows, until they are asked to go home, to be hidden from other men whose disgust is more in the acceptable human range.

I forced myself to look out of my own exalted window (fortieth floor, fortieth birthday). There was nothing but the familiar, spotty movement of cars and people; bugs and blurs. No violent crowds could be seen. The city was back to normal, as if it somehow knew I'd lied to Lester and returned him to it. The blurry city, shimmering under its twilight haze as it settled into its corruption, shining amid its filth, secured in its grime and dancing in its vile beauty— sending its magnificent stench up to the heavens—glittering, gleaming in its neon ooze of exquisite decay. (Rimbaud silent in the barbarism of his Africa, myself silent in this savage city.)

Chapter 35.   When I arrived at the airport to meet Carla's plane, hunger struck. I headed for the restaurant and destroyed a dozen plump clams, dipping them deep in a boisterous red sauce, and devoured them while thinking of the next course. Which turned out to be a massive marbled steak, charry on top but, once my teeth cut through, rare and ready to give up its juices. These mouthfuls I surrounded with gigantic chews of baked potato, dressed in sour cream and chives. Then, the first edge off starvation, I addressed myself to a piece of apple pie, some sour cheese and a pot of coffee, hot and bitter enough to wake the dead. Thus, both satisfied and stimulated, I found the waiting area at the gate where Carla's plane was scheduled to arrive, lay down on a bench and played with the idea of sleep.

But I was so tired that I could neither sleep nor stay awake. In the half-world between—behind my closed eyelids—I ran the credits. The day's experiment had been mine, but it was, still, in the great tradition of modernist experiments and credits must be allocated: Proust, Mann, Freud and his patients—all those who had invented the past. Behind them I came. And after me, perhaps thousands of people grasping their own lives, rejecting time, returning to revise events. From now on lives, like books, could be conceived in drafts. Nothing so fine that one could not add a few points. My day had been a beginning—crude, like all beginnings. It was only chance that I'd stumbled onto Stacey who'd taken her own life, eliminating all possibilities of revision. With a little care, such extremes could be avoided.

In my half-sleep I felt a sweet sense of rightness. Accepting no limits, blurring distinctions between reality and dreams, I'd been the André Breton of midtown Manhattan, the di Chirico of the middle class. Now, I thought with resignation, back to the Socialist Realism of my life. I awoke to find my wife bending over me.

"Hello," she said. "Happy birthday."

"How's your father?"

"Peeing like a charm. You look awful. How did you spend your birthday?"

I was, all at once, so glad to see her that I leaped up and grabbed her, laughing and whirling her around. "I didn't spend it! I still have it!" I shouted, whirling and laughing until she wept in my arms with fright.

Chapter 36.   I TRACKED her through the apartment as she touched things, straightening them, moving curtains to properly cover windows, putting a forgotten dish into the dishwasher. She was like a cat scratching at a corner to familiarize herself with it—to make sure it would serve as home.

"I'm being called for jury duty," I said.

"You should be exempt. You do it every day."

"Don't start. You seem different."

"How?"

"I don't know. I thought you'd have a suntan."

"California wasn't sunny this time. Besides, I was in the hospital, mostly."

In the bathroom, I watched her intently. She ignored the little diary with the blue fleur-de-lis. Instead she paused before the bathroom mirror on which was pasted my photograph, placed there a hundred years earlier, that morning. She pointed and said: "Why?"

"I woke up with birthday depression. So I thought I'd compare myself ten years ago or so with now."

"I think you compare well," she said. "But that may be because you're mine now. And because I was only fifteen years old then." She grinned.

A clue, I thought. Perhaps only our contemporaries are clear to us.

She added, deliberately trying to sound mischievous, "I have something to tell you. In bed."

But first came grilled cheese sandwiches and a story.

"I had a funny thing happen on the Sunset Strip," she said. "A kid, with his wife I guess—she had a baby in a kind of sling on her back—stopped me as I was coming out of a restaurant. A panhandler. Usually I can't stand them. But this one had such a wild and complicated story to tell, instead of the usual sob story, that I gave him five dollars. I was more surprised than he was."

"Five! What was the story?"

"All about how this was their wedding anniversary and they wanted to retrace every place and get back every experience they'd had in their married life—can't have been too long—all of two years, I think."

"But why the money?" I asked, not wanting to tell her yet about Bester's corps of fictioneers.

"Oh, a lot of stuff about being chased . . . it didn't matter after a while."

We laughed together with mouths full of melted cheese. Then I tore off my scrofulous clothes, took a steaming bath, and hit the bed to wait for Carla to finish her tub and to find out what she wanted to tell me in bed. I'd intended a loving, clean coupling to be next on the agenda. Except that she was so fatigued from her trip and the time change that I could not arouse enough sexual interest to make it all work.

"Don't now . . ." she murmured sleepily. "Let me tell you how I was riding in Mandeville Canyon and the sun slanted down into my eyes and I shut them and drove with my crazy eyes shut down that twisting road. All because I realized that you are terrific, you're my closed eyes, my ears, my voice, and I don't have to see everything, my darkness inside that is also very clear, you're my Abraham and Isaac and . . . ," her voice was trailing off into sleep with each syllable and the yellow smell of her hair was in my nose as I bent closer to hear what she was saying, ". . . and my sense of what it all is and is going to be and means and . . ."

Chapter 37.
THERE were flecks of soap on her right ear, the one next to my mouth. I blew them off and whispered: "Listen to the sound of my voice. Just listen. You are drowsy and you'll fall asleep as soon as I touch your ear at the count of three. And while you're asleep you'll listen . . ."

I paused.

"Yes . . ."

"You'll listen and do exactly what I ask."

"Yes."

"One . . . two."

"Mmm."

"Three."

"Mmmmmmmmmmmmmmm . . ."

I paused again, this time to assess what the hell I was doing. The pleasures of control after a buffeted day? Repeating my hypnosis in the park with poor Stacey, the day I was drafted? Nothing either so simple or arcane, I guessed. Just the chance to solve the mystery of my wife—that was all. Was that too much to ask? If I could Mesmer-Houdini-Freud my way into a wife's reality, who wouldn't follow me at the flicker of an eyelid? But, if I failed at such a large project, at least I could find out the meaning of the diary's words.

"Carla."

"Yes."

"'Late . . . If it's true I must do something about it.' What does that mean?"

A smile appeared from nowhere and settled on her entranced mouth.

"Bao silvari mane telero," she said.

It sounded vaguely like Portuguese. I remembered the circulars she'd received in the mail on returning from our honeymoon. Apparently she'd studied the language: but why? Would she, growing tired of life with a Jewish moralist, vanish some day into the Brazilian backland, some super-California even closer to natural sunny reality than any state in America could be?

To test her I asked her to repeat it. She did, flawlessly. It would seem I was married to a girl who spoke a terrific Portuguese. Even though it was getting more complicated instead of simpler, I continued. I was dogged.

"What does 'Late . . . must do something about it' mean?"

To my absolute amazement she answered in a perfectly exquisite voice I didn't know she owned.

It was Mahler—the last movement of the Fourth Symphony. Again, she was re-living the secret portions of our first year. All those records pouring in through the mails—and always Mahler or Delius, Berlioz or Elgar—every second-rate or, to be kind, second-rank composer who ever lived. Was she commenting on the foolishness of trying to re-make my life? That I would only have been second-rate if I'd persisted in music? A parody of Crown who was, himself, a parody of Beethoven? For a moment I was carried away by the thought of a world without major figures. For Germany, no Bach but von Dittersdorf. Or, to be generous, Spohr. For Russia, no Moussorgsky, only Liadov. A world in which Salieri *does* poison Mozart. Where would all my precious categories be then?

Or was there, in Carla's sweet singing, some other secret irony: a subtle statement that the whole notion of first- and second-rate was only typical of the pitiful categories invented by my Jewish, ethics-bound mind? And that if I listened freely to the lovely sounds she had just produced (and where did that tender *bel canto* come from? Had she been a diva in a previous life?) I would realize how irrelevant such terms were. All that was needed was to close one's eyes and listen.

But music, I quickly defended myself, asked nothing of us. Could one live as if the days and their responsibilities were music?

I was getting nowhere. A radical approach was called for. And since the root was and is the body I swept the covers from Carla and, still nurturing her trance, I tried to work my way into her secretive spirit via her equally secretive body.

Chapter 38. KNEELING at her side, I placed my hands on her feet.

"Feet," I said. And added, for greater clarity: "*Feet.*"

They were long and nicely flat, the bones well-articulated, the muscle that eventually led to the calf beginning quite high up so as not to spoil the elegance of the foot. The toes were small and with not too much differentiation, undramatic, the little toe very little and set far back from the others for an effect of delicacy.

I touched them. She responded in the simplest, clearest way, in a voice as sweet as that in which she'd just sung Mahler, suiting the response to the stimulus:

For feet: Feigned a limp to get out of going to school then fell and tore a ligament. Thus learning to believe in the power of language, of lying, of statement . . . Decided, in revenge, to become a dancer. But that didn't work out . . . Professor Stamitz said she was untalented. No rhythmic sense. Ran away from home over some unrecallable altercation with Mother (running, more feet) but came back in a few days.

I moved upward. "Legs," I said. They were long, tapered columns adding a sweep to the torso, strong but not visibly muscular.

"*Legs,*" I repeated.

For legs: At the high school prom she tore her stockings and hid in the Ladies' Room for an hour until a friend persuaded her to come back. Won the dancing contest that night. (No rhythmic sense Professor Stamitz?)

I touched her thighs, elegant conductors of muscle and sinew, first diminishing for shape and then growing fuller toward beginning buttocks.

"Thighs," I said.

For thighs: Was fat for a few years in adolescence . . . until she wrote away for a miracle diet and got back the thighs she wanted . . . and once when a boy called her frigid because she didn't respond to his desire to find out what lay at the juncture of her thighs, she'd held a kitten there and rocked and rocked until some sort of climax came, and she knew what the boy thought was wrong. (What the kitten thought, she had no idea.)

I was at her stomach now. Slightly rounded midpoint, a touch whiter than the breasts above, a light circle over the pubic exclamation point below.

"Stomach," I said.

For stomach: Two days before she was to leave Los Angeles for Sarah Lawrence (on a scholarship—they took her even though she couldn't really dance) she got awful stomach cramps. Appendicitis? No one knew. She'd photographed a lion cub and it had scratched her stomach right through her jacket, but that didn't seem to be the problem; it had healed all right. No one knew. They tested and tested—and finally it was too late for that term. And her mother, always superstitious, said she wasn't meant to go that far away from home and she had to go to college in San Bernardino where she could come home weekends. She yearned to get away to New York, to anywhere, and her stomach had held her home.

Past the chestbones, my hand moved to her breasts. Slightly rounded cones full of her youth, sensitive in the extreme to mouth and tongue.

"Breasts," I said.

For breasts: Finally made it to New York on a trip with her father—he was owner of a California vineyard—one of the early pioneers in getting good French grapes for American vineyards. She stayed on by effort of will and absence of Mother. She went to Doctor's Hospital to visit her mother's sister who'd had a mastectomy. (For days Carla had been holding off a man, probably Crown, from touching her breasts. After the shock of seeing her aunt, she went, all distracted, to a concert with Crown that night; when he touched her breast she went wild—slept with him.) So I knew what I'd suspected. Yet it felt, strangely, as if I knew

· 126 ·

nothing more than before. Or as if I'd always known. *Why is everything we learn touched with false surprise?*

My hand glided to her throat; an elegant column on which to seat her lovely head.

"Throat," I said, understandably anxious to change the subject.

For throat: It seemed the thing to do, to give up photography and become a model—abandon the active for the passive. But she stood next to those long-throated swan-models and dropped the idea.

I touched the corners of her sleeping mouth. If I could have induced an unconscious smile, I would have. It was a mouth sad in repose. But once the lips uncovered the bright, uneven teeth, an incredible lighting effect, from some invisible source, was induced; she smiled as lights shone. Could, indeed, shut it off as dramatically as that, as well.

For mouth: Didn't say a word until she was almost two years old. At seventeen had a miserable love affair and fell into a deep depression. One of the many California quacks suggested Malayan Deep Breathing—and it worked!

"Hands."

Fingers tapered to naturally luminescent nails—fluttering, expressive hands.

For hands: Burned in developing fluid . . . no scars . . . used them too much in acting class . . . ("Don't indicate, Carla. Feel!") Used to masturbate with one hand while touching her breast—sensitive nipple—with the other ("Don't *indicate*, Carla. Feel!")

For nose: In New York she lived in a hotel for girls, while going out with one Jewish intellectual after another. First Crown (and others) then me. There was a fire one night. Only Carla's sensitive nose sniffed out the first touch of smoke; she roused everyone and there were no casualties.

Except she stayed at the YMHA that night—and half-drowsing on a bench overheard part of a lecture on anti-Semitism in a room adjoining the lobby. It made her troubled about her father. (Speaking of noses.) Hers was a poised little upturn, a touch pink at the very end in all kinds of weather. *For eyes:* The truth of everything, since she watched her uncles paint, her brother manipulate an air-brush, since she could see. At the sanctimonious age of fourteen she announced at the dinner table that Man was corrupt—only animals were pure. The animal photographer was born. Had hysterical blindness for two months at the age of nine.

For vagina: The skipped-over area—saved for maximum effect, until the end. The night-mouth, the receiving, the accepting, the already-moist as I touched and slid a finger in a fraction of a millimeter to test the atmosphere. (*I'm telling you, Wolf, only Tessa can save you. Find her and shag the hell out of her . . . no matter . . .*) Ignoring that this was my wife, that she was under hypnosis, that she'd said no, earlier, I deliberately committed the silly sin of genteel, hypnotic rape. It was delicious in that night-mouth of hers, dark and full of sounds and sensations that made the whole experiment seem worthwhile. She responded precisely as she had on certain occasions when she'd had a little too much to drink or taken some minor drug she would, the next day, swear never to take again. Her sensuousness was muted. But I did not demand abandon on this particular occasion.

I came in her, neither of us protected against our fertility. Perhaps, months from now, she would be late and something—or nothing—would have to be done about it. Afterward I was like a man miraculously cured of a fever. Her body had indeed delivered her to me. She slept and I delighted in my new knowledge. It was so simple: she was a girl named Carla, born in the San Fernando Valley, where her father raised grapes, hated Jews, and chased women; where her mother worried herself into old age and she, Carla, longed to escape. Via college, love affairs, and an abortive career she *had* escaped to the big eastern city, and —to a Jewish husband. It was utterly familiar, American, traditional. As for the rest, we had years ahead of us to invent it. In the morning I would tell her everything that had happened. She would laugh at the right moments, be properly grave at certain points and would, finally, understand. It was never me who was the mysterious one anyway. Let the words remain unexplained. Not obscure or sinister, I thought drowsily, just unexplained.

And what of *my* secrets I thought, those I keep so well, or rather which keep themselves so well? What of my uncle in prison for embezzlement, my teacher at the seminary who'd kissed me on the mouth and then confessed love for me, throwing me into combined depression and exaltation for weeks? What of the gun my father kept in the bureau drawer, next to the pornographic pictures; the enormous and irrational pleasure I have always taken in the fall of snow? And my poor mother, half-mad by the age of thirty, leaving me little notes: *the rye bread is poisoned, eat only soup and be sure it's hot*—(heat kills, I know, dear Mother)— or: *all your trousers are torn, go naked today.* Poor lady who died so young, so full of love and trouble—the secret, perhaps, of all my secrets.

Chapter 39. No longer unknown, Carla slept. And I lay waiting for my own sleep which would not come. Well, I thought, as a professional moralist I would have to draw a moral. What had I learned? That the past is invention like the future. That the struggle is to prevent the present from becoming fiction? Barton had abandoned that struggle and practiced lunacy in a handsomely practical way. Crown, being an artist, had a different problem. But I —I'd lost a little ground and perhaps gained some. My days could still be mottled with many styles.

I'd told a lie and saved a man and taken my wife without her awareness or consent. And we were all probably a little worse and a little better for it. It was the kind of complicated but undramatic banality that Crown's contempt condemned me to: limbo. Not for me, apparently, a life in art, a life in hell.

Well, I'd once had my chance to control reality, to be the god of green grass and yellow suns and white clouds, to make Pastorales in music or words. My brief exhilaration was gone. It rushed over me with a terrible desolation, the magnificent chance I'd missed. *Not to have had a life.* To be an artist, instead. To abstract my life, to conceptualize it, to render it, to destroy and re-make it, to space it, to type it, to sing it, to word it, to rhyme it, to bind it, to finally syntactify it. Anything but live it! Only those who merely lived life out were condemned to pursue it as I had, along old streets which no longer led to the same corners, in old apartments which no longer contained the same passions, into the wild eyes of hunger strikers; and, at the last, down streets owned by the police, by the Mafia, and not by one's own imagination.

Chapter 40. I CLOSED my eyes against the feeling of defeat and, to seduce sleep, I drifted into the String Pastorale with which the day had begun. The violas pulsed and the violins swooped down on them as if in flight from the cellos. But I grew more ambitious. After all, had the years and the day taught me nothing? I added a brass choir for gravity, woodwinds for grace, percussion for punctation.

I found a place for Bester among the ambiguous oboes, neither sweet, like the flute I gave to poor Stacey, nor overpowering like the trombone to which I assigned my father. Tessa received a bassoon and I even found a place for the haphazard Sperber at the snare drum and a long, lyrical clarinet solo for Lester, who could barely summon the sustaining breath. Placing Piatigorsky in the First Cello chair and Crown behind the French horns I composed and conducted with all my brain and spirit.

It swept along beautifully as I tipped safely toward sleep and the dreams in which, as Doctor Savio has reminded us, all men are artists.

      . . . Like a dark rabbi, I
Observed, when young, the nature of mankind,
In lordly study. Every day, I found
Man proved a gobbet in my mincing world.
Like a rose rabbi, later, I pursued,
And still pursue, the origin and course
Of love . . .

                      —*Wallace Stevens*

About the Author   Daniel Stern is a
prominent author and literary critic whose essays appear in
Life, The Nation, The New York Times Book Review, and
Book World. He is the author of six highly praised novels:
*The Girl with the Glass Heart; The Guests of Fame; Miss
America: Who Shall Live, Who Shall Die; After the War;*
and *The Suicide Academy.* Mr. Stern has been a visiting
Fellow at the Center for the Humanities, Wesleyan Uni-
versity, and has lectured at many universities.